Guilty

Chris Barili

Guilty

Formatting by Rik - Wild Seas Formatting (http://www.WildSeasFormatting.com)
Cover art by Michelle Johnson of Blue Sky Design
Edited by Jennifer Severino

Printed in the United States of America

ACKNOWLEDGMENTS

Thanks to Jennifer Severino from Twitching Pen Editing, Rik Hall of Wild Seas Formatting (formatting), and Michelle Johnson of Blue Sky Designs (cover art). You guys made this book better than I ever could have without you.

DEDICATION

For KJ:

"For when she knocked on my door, then called me, she woke what had flowed dormant in my blood since her birth, so that what rose from the bed was not. . . any other. . .but the father of a girl."

Andre Dubus, A Father's Story

CHAPTER ONE

Frank opened his eyes to the rough, brown texture of the saloon's floorboards, his cheek stinging where it met the hewn surface of the wood. The gunshots had ceased, and the air bristled with tense silence.

He played dead for a moment to gather his wits. Something sticky had soaked through his shirt, and the room spun like he'd just tied one on.

After a moment, he pushed himself to his knees, plucking a splinter from just below his left eye. A pool of black ooze dripped like molasses through the floor boards. He found the same substance around a hole in the once white cotton of his shirt.

Still on his knees, Frank looked up. The inside of the saloon looked warped somehow. The swinging doors didn't line up right, like one had been mounted higher than the other. The picture window was wider at the bottom than the top, and seemed to tilt inward, as if shoved from the outside. The ceiling vaulted upward, its plastered surface too high for him to touch, even if he jumped.

"I didn't have *that* much to drink," he muttered under his breath.

He rose to one knee, wobbling on the uneven waves of the floor. Something passed so close to his shoulder it almost knocked him over. Roughly human in shape, it consisted of little more than an inky fog, like a heat shimmer had somehow turned black. It slid past him in silence and pushed through the uneven saloon doors, leaving them swinging.

Frank rubbed his eyes, a sudden pain piercing his temples. He'd been drinking at the bar. Whiskey, straight up. Cheap stuff, more like turpentine than righteous drink, but it worked. A bit too well, perhaps.

He'd hung his hat by the door—that much he remembered. His good hat, the black felt one, with the silk band and a crow's feather for luck. Sure enough, there it hung, faded to a storm-cloud gray. The crow's feather had been replaced by a pigeon's, dirty and pallid.

"What the Hell?"

"Nope, not Hell," came a husky voice behind him. "Not yet, anyway."

Spike Miller stood behind the bar, like he always did, but the familiarity ended there. A horn jutted from his forehead, erupting through bone and skin, leaving the surface cracked and bleeding. Spike had been an ugly cuss before, but now, he was downright hideous, with loose, flabby jowls, a pig snout, and large, dull teeth shining yellow in the dim light. His tiny, swine-like eyes gleamed wet, as if seeping fluid.

Frank reached for his six-gun, but Spike moved

faster. He pulled a double barrel shotgun from under the bar and held it under his own chin, stubby finger quivering on the trigger.

"I'll do it!" he shouted. "I'll blow my head off, Frank, if you so much as brush the ebony on that pistol's handle."

Frank glanced down at his Colt. The once ivory hand grips now gleamed black. He forced himself to inhale, then let it out in a long, measured sigh. He'd lost his mind.

"Why should I care if you shoot yourself, Spike?" he asked. "It might improve that ugly mug of yours."

"Because I know what's going on. You don't."

Another dark shadow-thing moved past Frank toward the door. He stepped out of its way, a chill running down his spine.

"Smart move." Spike lowered the shotgun and set it on the bar, patting it with sausage-like fingers. "Boss said something about two things not occupying the same space. Downright disastrous, he said."

"What are they?"

"They're my patrons," Spike answered. "Only they're back in the living world, and we're here, in between."

"In between?"

"Can't you figure it out, gunfighter?" He licked his thick, pink lips. "You were on the floor. In a puddle of blood. You're dead, Frank. Deader than Custer, Lincoln, and all them boys from the war."

Frank stuck his finger in the hole in his shirt. His fingertip went through his ribcage and into the cavity of his chest.

He went numb.

"Who shot me?"

"Marshal Redding," Spike replied. "Stumbled on you. Got the drop before you even knew he was there. You went for your piece, but..."

Frank remembered. He'd been too slow. He'd known a split second before he'd touched his pistol that he was going to die, but he'd tried anyway. He'd gotten careless. Lazy and drunk. And he'd paid for it.

"So, this is Heaven, then?" he asked.

Spike snorted a laugh, and a gob of green shot from his nose, landing on the bar to slither away in a trail of slime.

"Heaven?" Spike slapped the bar with his meaty hand. "You think Heaven is a rundown saloon in Tombstone? I think that bullet messed with your brain, Frank."

He picked up a filthy cloth and wiped up the slime trail.

"So, I'm in Hell, then. Should've known. Never could get a fair shake."

Spike shook his head and slithered around the end of the bar. Seeing Spike's body made Frank's heart run like a wild pony. The bartender's arms connected to a plump, fatty torso, wrinkled and folded, with low-hung teats and a whiskey-barrel gut bulging under his shirt. From the waist down, he looked like a slug, a tapering of the same fat body.

Spike must have caught him looking, for he paused, then shrugged and moved to Frank's side.

"Apologize for my appearance," he said. "I took the form of someone familiar to you, but Spike's body didn't change well."

"No, it sure didn't. Now, you gonna tell me what's going on?"

"That's right hard to explain, Frank. Think of this as your personal purgatory, populated with your nightmares. You're stuck here until the judges decide your fate. You killed a whole herd of men in your lifetime, four of them unjustly. You'll face those four and one justified kill here. The judges will weigh your heart and determine if the one justified kill outweighs the four unjust ones."

Frank hadn't thought much on the men he'd killed. It wasn't good business for a gunfighter to reminisce. The past wouldn't kill you, but the future sure could. And in Frank's case, it had.

"They all deserved it," he replied, patting the pistol at his hip. "I didn't kill anyone who didn't need to die."

Even as he said it, his voice sounded hollow, like an empty casket.

"I reckon that's the judges' decision. You're being arraigned tonight. There's a coach waiting outside."

"And if I don't go?"

"Then you're stuck here for eternity, Frank,

reliving your killings over and over, each one worse than the last. We change things here, make them harder. We make sure you see the truth, so reliving is a thousand times harder than living was."

Frank didn't like the sound of that. "Who sits in judgment? God? Satan?"

Spike laugh-snorted again, ejecting another ball of green that stuck to Frank's sleeve. Frank swiped at it, but the glob jumped to Spike's outstretched hand. Spike lifted the thing to his face and let it crawl back inside his nose with a slurp.

"Neither," Spike replied, wiping his nose on his sleeve. "They're too busy, so they delegate. I can't say who your judges will be, but they'll be suited to your case."

"I'm innocent," Frank argued. "This ain't even close to fair."

Spike studied him a moment, his tiny pig eyes wet. Then he shrugged and slithered toward the door.

"You'd better move along," he said, holding open one of the doors. "Time's a-wasting."

CHAPTER TWO

If the saloon had made Frank dizzy, the street threatened to drive him mad. Black shadows moved everywhere, and Frank danced to avoid them. To his left, the bank building swayed as if in a heavy wind. Across the sepia-colored dirt of Allen Street, the Cochise Hardware Store shimmered behind a curtain of light, and to its left, the OK Corral stood draped in swirling black.

"That place is always dark." Frank spun and came face to face with an Indian man, face war-painted. He wore no shirt, his biceps bulging inside bands of multi-colored beads. His waist ended in fur where his hips should have been, his lower half that of a dog or wolf. A long, scraggly tail dragged in the dirt, matted and dusty.

"Who the Hell are you?" Frank asked. "Or rightly, what the Hell are you?"

The Indian thought for a moment, then smiled. "I am Batcho, your guide and lawyer."

Behind him, a stagecoach waited, its windows glowing red, like Hell itself rode inside. Two things that had once been horses pulled the coach, skin and fur falling to the ground like dust, exposing sinew and bone underneath. One of them pawed at the ground, stirring up a dust devil.

Seated on the driver's bench was a figure in a black duster and a black hat with a wide, sweeping brim. The figure turned to look at him, and Frank felt like an icy blade had pierced his heart. Where a face should have been, darkness swirled, a cloud of midnight much like the one that enveloped the OK Corral. Two pinpoints of yellow gleamed amidst the blackness. The sound of a whip cracked the air, making Frank jump and reach for his piece. But the driver didn't move, and Frank forced himself to relax.

"Who made an Indian my lawyer?" Frank asked.

"The court, of course," Batcho answered. He motioned to the coach. "Please get in. Your time is limited."

"You want me to ride in that?" Frank took another step back.

Batcho shrugged, his smile fading. "You must."

Frank's gut twisted, but he had no choice. Sighing, he mounted the coach. The Indian climbed in beside him and rapped on the ceiling. Again, the whip sound split the air around them, and the stage leapt forward. Frank found himself pushed back in his seat, breathing labored. Outside his window, Allen Street streaked by and black shadows jumped out of the way with muffled shouts.

In seconds, they thundered past a row of

Chinese tenements, and then they cleared the town, barreling west toward the mountains. Out the window, Frank watched the hills fly past, looking like slumbering beasts in the distance. He shivered when one raised its head, maw dripping.

At some point, he fell asleep and awoke to Batcho slapping his shoulder.

"Get down, Frank Butcher," his Indian guide said. "On the floor, before they see you."

Frank paused, unable to gather his thoughts. Outside the Indian's window, the Sonoran desert streamed past, a twisted landscape of yellows, browns, pinks, and reds that either reflected the sky or were reflected in it. Ahead of them, the sun set, blood red and dripping onto the horizon, like the sky had been shot and lay dying over the earth. Movement caught his eyes. Something dark ran parallel to the coach, slipping in and out of sight as if passing behind trees that didn't exist. Bright, red eyes and fangs as long as daggers flashed in the dim light.

Batcho shoved Frank to the floor and threw an old blanket over him.

"Do not move," he commanded.

Frank felt a presence at his window, cold and reeking of death and fear. He forced himself to lie still while Batcho said something in his native tongue. A growling, hissing voice replied, oozing with anger and rage. Batcho spoke again, and the presence felt closer, larger, right outside the stage.

As fast as it came, it disappeared. Frank started

to move, but Batcho kicked him through the blanket, so he stayed still. After what seemed an eternity, the Indian ripped the blanket off, and Frank squinted against the slanting sunlight.

"What was that?" he asked, climbing back into the seat, but shrinking himself as small as possible.

"Hellhound," Batcho replied. His tail flicked, tense. "They hunt this desert at dusk and dawn."

"And if they'd seen me?"

"You would have missed your arraignment forever. If you die in the underworld, you remain here for eternity. Rule number one in this place: you must survive."

Frank was about to ask more when the coach slowed. Batcho smiled again, his eyes sparkling gold.

"We are here," he announced.

The sky darkened in minutes as the sun dropped below the horizon. As the last rays winked out, a twisted line of dancing orange light sliced through the dark desert floor like an angry scar. A river flowed south to north, flames jumping on its surface. Frank tensed as the stage clattered onto a wooden bridge over the flaming water.

"You know this river?" Batcho asked.

"Nope. Never seen a river of fire before."

"Look closer, Frank Butcher."

They rolled off the bridge on the far bank, then turned north. Before long, they stopped and Batcho opened the door. Frank stepped out and found himself before a great stone structure perched on a cliff over the river. They faced a Sally Port with a raised portcullis.

"Yuma Territorial Prison," Frank muttered. "Well I'll be—"

He let the sentence trail off, afraid it touched too close to the truth.

"Now, do you know the river?" Batcho asked.

"The Colorado. Why's it on fire?"

"This is not the world of the living. Things here are worse. Now, come."

The portcullis clanged closed behind them, and they hurried across a courtyard to rows of crude, stone cells. As they passed, growls and moans clawed their way through the iron mesh doors, punctuated by screams of agony. Frank jumped as something hissed to his left, and again when a shadow lunged at him from the right.

They came to a wall carved into a hillside that climbed to a watch tower above. Frank recognized the single narrow door before them.

"The dark cell," he said. "So, I spend eternity in the dark cell until I go mad?"

"No, Frank Butcher," said Batcho. "The judges wait inside. If they find your heart is pure, you will go to the new territory and forget your suffering. If they find your heart dark, you will spend eternity in the fiery deserts of Hell."

"I can't appeal?"

"There is one way, but pray we do not need it. Most do not survive. Hurry now. The judges wait."

"Nothing like hurrying to your damnation,"

Frank muttered.

His stomach in a knot, Frank pushed open the door and stepped inside.

An inner door of iron mesh stood open, allowing him access to the pitch-black chamber. Batcho guided him to the right, through another door, then stopped him.

Three shapes stood before him, all at least seven feet tall, with broad shoulders and heads bowed under brimmed hats.

"Your honors," Batcho began, "may it please the court, I represent the late Mister Franklin D. Butcher, gunfighter, murderer, gambler, and outlaw. He enters a plea of not guilty."

The judges looked up, their eyes blazing under the brims of their hats: blue on the left, green on the right. But the eyes of the middle judge glowed red hot and baleful, fiery embers embedded in his skull. Those eyes burned at Frank with pure hatred.

"It does not please us!" All three spoke as one, their layered voices echoing in perfect unison off the chamber walls of. "He is a loveless man, with hate in his heart. Many have died by his hand, four were innocent. Let him rot in Hell!"

"Surely, your honors, there must be some good in this man. Many who died by his bullets deserved their fate. He has rid the world of robbers, killers, and evil men. Does that not outweigh his sins?"

The flames behind the judges leapt higher, singeing Frank's face. The judges loomed nearer, towering over them.

The middle judge spoke alone this time, his ember eyes flaring with every word.

"He took innocent lives! Nothing outweighs that!"

"I feared it would come to this," Batcho whispered to Frank. Then, he turned to the judges. "My client requests trial by testing."

This time, the voices rang like bells, making Frank cover his ears. "He dares to challenge our authority?"

"He doesn't mean—"

Frank cut the Indian off with a wave of his hand.

"I challenge your judgment," he said. Batcho gasped. "You don't know me. You ain't never met me. I never killed anyone who didn't deserve it, and I'll prove it. You'll see."

All three pairs of eyes flared at him. The judges stood even taller, and flames crackled and smoked behind them. Now, Frank could see the judges' silhouettes, each one wearing a long, black duster. One held a rifle, while the other two cast open their dusters to reveal six-guns on their hips. Badges gleamed on their chests.

For an instant, Frank heard only hissing, like the room crawled with vipers, as the judges conferred. A moment later, all three faced him.

"You will be tried by testing, Frank Butcher," they replied, "as your father was before you. Your attorney will explain the rules. Breaking them will condemn you to eternity here, where you will relive your killings in agony forever. Now, leave us."

"My father? What do you know—"

"Be gone!" their voices thundered, shaking dust from the ceiling. "Before we change our minds!"

Batcho dragged Frank from the room.

* * *

Back in the courtyard, beyond the horrifying cell blocks, Batcho leaned against the blackened bones of a tree.

"You took a big chance, Frank Butcher. The judges do not tolerate disrespect."

"They're wrong. Those men all deserved killing."

Batcho shook his head. "You do not understand. Of the five men you must face, all but one were innocent. You cannot argue that. You will fight versions of all five. You must kill only the one who truly deserved death. That will prove your heart has changed. Fail, however—kill even one of the innocents—and you will burn in Hell forever. If the things in this prison scare you, what hunts the plains of Hell will freeze your blood.

"If you fail to complete your testing, you cannot be judged. You will spend eternity here, reliving your killings a million times over, haunted by your sins. If you die here, you will be deemed guilty."

Frank scratched the stubble on his chin. "What happened to my father?"

Batcho shrugged. "I did not represent him. I do not know."

Of course. "So, they appointed you, but told you nothing?"

"Not they, Frank Butcher. He. The Chief Justice. With the red eyes."

Frank sighed. That one had it in for him—this testing would not be fair.

They boarded the stage, the driver cracked his invisible whip, and they were off. Ahead of them, the burning river stretched into the distance right and left, a line of orange light growing as they approached. Halfway across the bridge, they clattered to a stop, and Batcho climbed out onto the timbers of the bridge. Frank followed, and they stood at the rail, watching the fiery river flow backward.

"Your first test is here," Batcho said. "In Yuma. Where you killed your last man."

Frank remembered. "I didn't kill him near the river, so why are we stopped here?"

"Before you are tested," Batcho explained, "you must remember. Our way."

Frank felt rather than saw the driver appear behind him. He spun, but too late. The driver shoved him over the rail.

He hit the water head first, splashing through the flames, striking a rock on bottom. He gasped, and water flooded his lungs. Scalding hot, it burned his throat and seared his mouth. Frank fought to find the surface, kicking and thrashing, but he couldn't tell which way was up. He tried to look, but the water burned his eyes.

He couldn't stop himself from choking now, couldn't expel the boiling water. He gasped, and more fire entered his body. He felt himself dying, slipping into darkness as the water burned and charred him from the inside out. A moment later, darkness claimed him.

CHAPTER THREE

He sits at the table, cards close to his vest, watching the fat man across from him. A spittoon on the floor reeks of chew and consumption. He peeks at his hand—three kings, a four, and a two. He tosses another five dollar chip on the pile.

"Call." His voice drowns in piano music, the only other sound in the room.

Across from him, the fat man's face shows nothing, his double chin motionless as smoke curls around his head. Gold rings sparkle on his fingers.

Frank has him beat. There's no way the gambler has more than two pair. With almost a hundred dollars riding on it, Frank knows he's right.

The rest of the saloon is eerily quiet. The piano falls silent. A hooker on a rancher's lap pauses mid-sentence, painted mouth open. Even a cowhand sitting alone in a corner stares. The entrance doors squeak in the Yuma breeze, while out of sight, a woman coughs, a wet, wracking sound that makes the dealer jump.

The fat man lays down, his bowtie mouth curling up in a smile.

"Full house, aces over fours."

Frank's gun is out before the cards hit the table. The fat man puts his hands up, but his smile doesn't change.

"Now, now, Mister Butcher," he says, "don't be a sore loser. I won this fair and square, so pay up like a gentleman."

"You're a cheat," Frank replies, his Colt aimed at the gambler's chest. The saloon empties but for the barkeep and the gambler's "personal assistant," a skinny boy with rat-like eyes. "Roll up your sleeves, fat man."

The gambler stands, tugs at the velvet lapels of his purple suit coat, then at the white cuffs sticking out from the sleeves. Gold buttons run down the middle of his chest, and the slide clasp of his bolo tie looks tiny against his broad waddle.

"I will do no such thing, sir."

He eyes his pistol—a British revolver—on the table.

"Don't," Frank warns. "Now, roll up those sleeves or die."

The assistant moves back a step, wringing his hands. The gambler lets out a great sigh, enough to rustle the cards on the table, then removes his coat and hangs it on the back of his chair. His belly is gigantic, and the buttons on his shirt strain, as if some great beast fights for escape. He rolls up his right sleeve, his pudgy fingers fumbling with the button, then the left. His flabby arms are hairless, but no cards fall out.

Frank approaches the chair, forcing the gambler back, away from the table.

"I'm an honest player," says the gambler.

"Then, why were there five aces in that deck?"

The cheater stammers. In the back, a woman hacks again.

"You slipped in an extra four, too. The four of clubs came out twice this game."

"You were counting cards, sir. You are the cheat!"

Frank steps forward and points his Colt at the man's face.

"No law against arithmetic." He plucks the coat off the man's chair and shakes it. An ace falls from the left sleeve. "But that there's cheating, you fat son of a bitch."

The assistant runs from the room, and the barkeep ducks behind the bar.

The gambler drops to his knees, jowls jiggling.

"Please, Mister Butcher, show mercy. You can have the money. Just don't shoot me. I have—"

Frank fires at point-blank range. The man's head snaps back, and he falls, shaking the entire room when he hits. Frank scoops up the cash and runs out the back. A woman's hacking cough chases him from the saloon.

* * *

Burning. All over his body, like flames had seared him from his lungs outward. He kicked and writhed and rolled, trying to put out the fire, but it did no good. He still burned.

"Frank Butcher!" Someone slapped his cheek. "Wake up!"

The flames subsided a bit, and Frank opened one eye. The sun beat down, scorching his skin. He lay on his side on the barren, gravelly ground, out of the river. And he wasn't on fire, though it sure felt like flames danced a jig on his skin.

"Are you well?" Batcho looked down at him, the sun forming a golden halo behind his head. "Frank Butcher?"

Frank groaned and rolled onto his back. The sky had turned a pale purple, the sun a golden disk suspended in it like a button on the fat man's suit coat. Behind Batcho, the stage waited, the driver oblivious to the heat.

"We must go," Batcho said. "The coach waits."

Frank sat up, his head swimming. He took inventory of his body, checking everything he could see. Nothing appeared burned, not even the hair on his arms. By all rights, he should be dead. Then he remembered being pushed and sprang to his feet. He grabbed the Indian by his hair and yanked him up as well.

"You set me up!" he shouted, pulling back his fist.

Batcho didn't flinch. "I did not. My instructions were to show you the river. I didn't know the driver would...do that."

Frank glared at the driver and reached for his pistol. Batcho stopped him with a hand on his elbow.

The driver turned his head, his eyes blazing under the turned-down brim of his hat. Frank's resolve faded.

"I suppose I ain't hurt." He relaxed and looked into Batcho's gold-brown eyes. "Next time, warn me. You're supposed to be my guide. So, guide."

The red man nodded, and they boarded the stage.

"Did you learn anything from the river?" Batcho asked.

Frank remembered what he'd seen. It had been perfect, every detail, right down to the coughing and the smell and the fat man's jiggling flesh. Frank had never dreamed about this kill before, but he'd never fallen in a river of fire, either.

"I remembered," he said, staring out his window as the purple-and-orange desert streaked past outside. "I remembered the last man I killed."

Batcho nodded. "Then, the learning will come."

A few minutes later, they pulled into Yuma, slowing to a trot to allow the black shadows to get out of the way.

"Can they see us?" Frank asked.

Batcho scratched his smooth chin. "When you were alive, did you ever feel like you were being watched? Ever have a feeling that you weren't alone?"

Frank nodded.

"That is how they 'see' us in the living world," Batcho went on. "Premonition, bad feelings, unexplained knockings. Things that steal sleep. We are less visible in their world than they are here, but we're still present."

Frank had never been superstitious. He'd always ignored things like that as his mind playing tricks on him. Now he wondered what else he'd been wrong about.

Yuma burned like the river had. Flames leapt from rooftops, out of windows, and across balconies. Burning trees billowed black smoke, darkening the sky. Frank coughed, and Batcho covered his mouth with a kerchief.

For all their heat and smoke, though, the flames didn't consume. Buildings stood, walls uncharred. Leaves still blew in the wind, curtains still billowed, even wrapped in fire. Even the sky here had turned a mix of fire orange, ember red, and soot black.

They drew up in front of the saloon. Fire danced inside its windows, and its swinging doors burned. Frank tied his own kerchief over his nose and mouth, blocking out some of the smoke.

They stepped out.

"You must go alone," Batcho said. "Remember, only one of the men you'll face again deserved it, and I don't think the judges would pit you against him first. There are more tests."

"This kill was justified," Frank said. "Now, let me get this over with."

He put his hand on his pistol, comforted by the familiar kiss of cold steel, and climbed the steps to the swinging doors.

The doors parted without even a touch, and the sounds of the saloon spilled out into the street. The clang of an out-of-tune piano tumbled over him. Laughter and the clink of glasses joined the music. Over them all, a woman coughed.

Frank stepped inside, and all noise stopped, plunging the bar into silence. Death's silence. The fat gambler sat at the table, his beady eyes glaring over a fan of cards. Nothing else about him was the same. His body took up an entire side of the table, his bulbous head purple and spotted. In place of his nose and mouth was a beak, snapping. Eight purple arms waved around him, each holding a fan of cards, and a foot-high deck sat on the table. The assistant's pointed nose twitched, wiggling his whiskers, and a long, thin tail wrapped around him. The dealer seemed normal enough, dressed as Frank had last seen him. The only other occupant was a thin, naked woman standing in the doorway to the back room. Her emaciated body looked like a skeleton with leather stretched over it. Her sunken blue-gray eyes met Frank's, and she hacked, her whole chest caving in. She spat brown phlegm into a spittoon with a clang.

Frank paused. Something about her shook his confidence, made him wonder about his certainty in this kill.

"Well, if it isn't Mister Butcher," the gambler said. He clacked his beak, as if biting off a chunk of meat. "Let's play a hand or two."

"Or eight?" Frank didn't bother masking the

dislike in his voice.

Flames roared behind the bar, and the ceiling blazed. Sweat ran down Frank's neck, but he nodded and moved to the chair opposite the gambler.

"Deal me in," he said.

The dealer's hands never moved. He simply looked at Frank and five cards appeared on the table before him. And so it began. The gambler won the first hand, Frank the next two, as it had gone in life. Frank lost himself in the games, in the numbers and math of counting cards. He saw his cards and the gambler's giant purple face, nothing more. He watched several times as the fat man pulled cards from one of his eight sleeves, but he said nothing. He had to play this just right if he wanted absolution.

The woman coughed -- a horrendous, tearing hack that sounded like her lungs were ripping from her chest.

"For crying out loud, woman," the gambler shouted, "take your sickness back to your room. None of us want it."

The woman stood, watching Frank with flat, accusing eyes that chipped even more off the block of his confidence. What was it about her?

They played and played, replaying every hand as they had before, the gambler cheating on most and still losing as many as he won. When they came to the final hand, the one Frank had dreamed about, Frank forced himself to breathe.

The gambler raised the ante, and Frank tossed in the chip to match it.

"Call."

Counting cards had done him no good, with several hundred cards in the deck, but he still knew what each of them would play. Of that, he had no doubt.

He laid down his three kings, watching the gambler, who somehow managed to grin, the corners of his beak turning up. He slid a card from his sleeve and slipped it into his hand. Frank knew what came next, but felt like he'd missed something important. He glanced at the woman, but she hadn't moved. Her eyes still bore into him, twin pits of shadow and gloom.

"Who is she?" he asked before the gambler could play.

"Who?"

"The woman with the pretty voice."

The gambler looked back at the woman, and his grin changed to a frown. The fire behind the bar flared, and the ceiling fire seemed lower, hotter. It dripped tiny gobs of fire on the floor.

"She's my wife," the fat man answered. "Has the consumption, I'm afraid. I play to win money to keep her medicated. She doesn't have too much longer, and I want her to be comfortable."

Frank's composure dropped for an instant. The judges were right about this one. He never should have shot him.

"Then, I suppose you should play your hand,"

Frank said.

The gambler's eyes narrowed. A tiny flame dripped to the table, and Frank patted it out with his hat.

The gambler laid down three fours, a king and a jack.

Frank looked up in surprise. The gambler rose, his massive purple body shoving the table back, beak snapping.

"You're a rotten cheat!" he hissed.

Each of his eight hands held a British revolver, all of them aimed at Frank. Frank flipped the card table and dove behind it as shots rang out. He rolled to his left and crawled behind the bar, bullets ricocheting around him. Glass shattered and rained down as he crouched just inches from a fire burning there. When the shooting stopped, Frank jumped up, pistol in his hand, and fired all six rounds. His shots were true—they always were—each one taking off an arm, leaving the gambler with two.

The gambler went to aim his remaining pistols, but before he could, his body warped and twisted. Frank watched as the monster disappeared, and before him stood the gambler, as he'd known him in life, flabby and pale.

Frank ducked, reloaded, and stood, aiming his pistol at the other man's head. The gambler sat on the floor, cradling one of the lost tentacles, tears streaming down his face. His pistols lay silent on the floor.

"We're not so different, you and me," he said.

"We both cheated. The difference is that I cheated for her. You did it for yourself."

For a moment, Frank stood, his Colt aimed at the gambler's head. His finger twitched on the trigger, longing to fire the shot that would kill the man again. Instead, he holstered his piece, looked the gambler in the eye, and pointed to the ante scattered on the floor.

"It's all yours," he said. "I won't need it."

He strode from the saloon.

CHAPTER FOUR

The stage rumbled across the night-darkened desert with Frank collapsed inside, head against the doorframe, eyes closed. The hacks of the gambler's wife echoed in the dark recesses of his mind. He hadn't known in the living world that the gambler needed the money for her treatment.

He wondered if it would have made a difference.

"He still cheated," he told Batcho.

"Who took care of her after he died?" the red man asked.

"I don't care."

"No one. She died in agony a year later in a back alley of Yuma. Alone."

Frank punched the padded wall.

"I did what your judges wanted," he said. "They excuse cheating, so I spared the gambler. So, where now?"

"Albuquerque," the Indian said, looking out his own window. "The Rio Grande. You remember that place, don't you?"

Frank grunted, trying to drudge up some

memory. He scoured his brain, searching for what had happened there, but he found dark patches where memories should have been.

"Did I kill someone there?"

Batcho's thin, brown lips bent downward at the corners. His brow creased.

"Think, Frank Butcher. You must remember."

Frank looked out the window, but memory wouldn't come. No matter how deep he dug, it seemed that he only scratched the surface. Frustrated, he fell asleep to the sound of coughing in his mind.

When he woke, sunlight streamed through the windows of a coach. An Indian snored on the seat across from him. Outside, the sun lit a landscape of odd shapes and indistinct colors, like everything had blurred together. A saguaro melted into a vague greenish blob, and the sun was little more than a cloudy fog of yellow. It made Frank queasy.

The coach slowed, waking the Indian.

"Are we there yet?" he asked, rubbing his eyes.

"Where?"

"Albequerque. You killed a man here."

Frank shrugged. He had no memory of killing someone, no memories at all.

"Did I? I'd remember that."

"You forgot already, Frank Butcher?" the Indian asked him. "That is the Rio Grande clouding your mind, but you will remember. You must."

When the stagecoach stopped, the Indian opened the door and hopped down. As soon as he left the coach, his features blurred, and by the time Frank joined him, he was little more than a brown smear on an ambiguous background. The blur pointed to a river. At least, Frank thought it was a river. It looked like a thin, brown worm slinking across a pastel painting.

"Go," said a familiar voice. Frank squeezed his eyes tight and tried to picture the face it belonged to, but could not. "The river has what you need. Drink."

Desperate to remember, Frank ran to the river's bank, but it too was blurry, and he over-shot. He fell, muddy water flooding around him, seeping into his nose and ears. An instant later, it filled his mouth and everything went black.

* * *

A hooker sits on his knee, her overdone makeup a mask so perfect, he can't even remember her name. Her blonde curls tumble to her shoulders, parting to let a mole peek out at the nape of her neck.

He ignores the urge to kiss the mole. His eyes wander down to her ample cleavage, spotting another mole down where he can't see it all. But he wants to.

"Enjoying the view?" she asks. Her breathy voice, close to his ear, drowns out the sounds of a cheap piano and laughter, but it cannot silence the nagging voice of warning in his head.

"I've seen better," he lies. "Hills outside Yuma

are younger, probably firmer, and mountains around Gunnison are bigger."

Her jaw drops, and she gives him a playful slap on the chest, letting her hand linger there. She smells of lilac, cigar smoke, and sex. She leans across him to pick up her drink from the table.

Frank tosses down his tumbler of whiskey and pats her bottom with his other hand. He feels the curve of her buttock on his thigh, feels himself harden.

"Oh, Mister Butcher," she says, fanning herself. "It's getting warm in here. Let's retire to your room, where we can open the window."

He nods, and she jumps off his leg. He orders another whiskey as they pass the bar.

In his room, a Winchester 73 leans against the window sill. The whiskey makes his head spin, makes him forget why he is here. He wanders to the open window, looks out at Second Street. His horse remains hitched below. The street whirls like a calliope, and Frank starts to fall.

She grabs him, pulls him back, and pushes him against the wall. The Winchester clatters to the floor as she presses her soft body against him and engulfs his mouth in a waxy kiss.

His hand wanders from her waist to her bottom, pulling her hips against his.

A horse whinnies outside. Frank shoves what's-her-name back and wheels to the window. Below, a young, slender man struggles to mount Frank's skittish horse.

"Horse thief!" Frank yells, grabbing the Winchester and chambering a round. He aims, and the boy looks up, one foot in the stirrup. He's half Indian, with a hook nose and fierce, dark eyes. Frank feels like he knew him long ago, in another lifetime. But he can't quite place him.

He shakes himself as the boy gains the saddle. Without a horse, a man isn't a man. So, as the boy fights to control the stomping, kicking gelding, Frank aims for the spot between the shoulder blades. He fires.

The boy straightens, his arms scrabbling at his back like he can pull the bullet out, and he tumbles from the saddle. Frank drops the rifle, draws his Colt, and runs from the room.

The dirt of the street drinks in the boy's blood as Frank re-hitches his horse. Kneeling, he rolls the boy over, and again feels a twinge of familiarity.

"How old are you?" he asks, a crowd gathering behind him.

"Fourteen," the boy chokes. A pang of regret bites at Frank's heart. Frank did stupid things at that age, too.

"Stealing a horse is a death offense."

The boy nods. Sure enough, he has some Indian in him, this one. His hair is not quite black, his skin not quite red.

"My Ma," the boy coughs. "Over at the Indian school. Wanted me to grow up like my dad, more like a white man. Give her this."

He presses a leather pouch full of coins into

Frank's hand, then his eyes close, and his breathing stops.

Frank rises and backs away, holstering his pistol with a trembling hand. This doesn't feel like his other kills, doesn't give him a rush of exhilaration. Instead, it fills him with a dark cloud of dread that chills his soul.

He shakes his head. The law would have hung the boy, so Frank just saved them the trouble.

The hooker appears at his side, her hand out. "I'll give it to her," she says.

She'll probably spend it on cheap perfume and liquor, but what would he tell the grieving mother?

"I shot your boy, but he left you some coins. Have a nice day."

Frank jumps into the saddle and gallops from Albuquerque, a bottle in his hand. By sunup, he's forgotten about the hooker, the coins, and the boy.

* * *

Frank dragged himself up the low river bank, spitting gritty water on the still, brown grass. Exhausted, he fell on his belly, trying to remember where he was.

"Frank Butcher, you must get up."

He raised his head and looked into the deep, golden eyes of an Indian man whose lower half looked like a dog. He knew this creature, did not fear him, but did not know his name. His mind seemed filled with fog, swirling and leaving him directionless. The Indian handed him a canteen.

"Fill this. You will need it."

Frank kneeled and filled the canteen where the river looked clearest. As the water washed over his fingers, a name came to his mind.

"Batcho," he muttered. "Your name is Batcho."

"We must go," said the red man. "We must reach Albuquerque soon. Your next test is there."

The Indian put his hands under Frank's armpits and hauled him to his feet. Frank studied the landscape. The river ran behind him, with open desert on either side. Sand stretched away, blurring as it went. Ahead of him, a large, red brick building sat under the rising sun. It looked as if someone had picked it up from a city block and dropped it beside the river.

"The Albuquerque Indian School," his guide told him. "Do you remember it?"

Frank shook his head. He knew he should remember, but his mind drew a blank. Outside the building, Indian children played tug-o-war or tetherball, or simply chased each other in their dirty, gray uniforms. A rail-thin Indian woman with a hook nose and stringy, black hair stood by the wall, watching them pass. Her fierce, dark eyes looked familiar, like he'd seen them in a dream but had woken up before he saw the rest of her.

The low outline of Albuquerque materialized from simple, dark shapes into buildings, dull grays and browns in the morning sunlight. As they entered town, a sign read Silver Street. It seemed all but deserted, the sound of their footsteps echoing down the canyon of a street.

They passed Second Street, and a hotel loomed over them. A saloon on the first floor stood silent, though light and motion spilled out, beckoning for him to enter.

"Hotel Columbus," Frank read. "I know this place. I think this is—"

"No, Frank Butcher," said his companion. "This place is not for you."

Something made Frank stop, tugging on an invisible rope hitched to his thoughts. Batcho edged away from him, continuing east a few steps. Then, he stopped, tail twitching.

Frank unslung the canteen from his shoulder and raised it to his lips.

"This is not the time," said the Indian. His eyes darted from Frank to the hotel and back.

Frank ignored him and took a sip of the Rio Grande's gritty waters.

A swollen river of memories flooded his mind. Frank fought to control himself, to stay planted while the visions washed over him.

Piano music, whiskey, black lace. Cheap lipstick on his face, golden curls tumbling down his chest, a firm rump in his hand.

"I need to go inside."

Frank stomped up the rickety wooden steps. Batcho followed close behind, tail whipping side to side in protest.

Inside, the feeling of lost familiarity tugged even harder, cementing Frank's belief that he needed to be here. He moved to a dusty bar stool and sat, leaning an elbow on the bar.

"There is nothing here, Frank Butcher."

A row of brown and white bottles lined a shelf behind him, their labels blurry and unreadable. A layer of dust coated the mahogany bar top, and cobwebs hung in corners.

Maybe the Indian was right. Nothing here meant anything to him. He rose to go, catching a glimpse of himself in the mirror, and suddenly, the feeling of faded memory overpowered him.

He opened the canteen and took a deep pull.

The room erupted in noise. Someone poked away at a piano, while men laughed. Glasses clinked. A woman whispered in his ear, her breath warm against his neck. But around him, nothing else changed.

He took another swallow.

Color exploded—red, yellow, black, and gold—and he saw them all. The bartender stared at him. Five men appeared, playing poker around a table, while two more drank in a back corner. A hooker appeared on his lap, her ridiculously red lips pursing.

Frank remembered it all. The bar, the hooker, the whiskey, and the way his head swam from the booze. He had been here, and he knew what would happen next. The hooker stood, curls bouncing, and tugged him up the stairs.

The Winchester leaned against the wall, and a horse whinnied on the street below. Frank went to the window and leaned out into the cool, dry air. On the street, a young, fierce-eyed boy struggled with a horse, trying to climb into the saddle while the gelding skipped about.

Frank needed to do something, but he didn't know what. As he watched, the sounds and sights started to fade.

Confused, Frank moved back from the window. The light dimmed, sounds became muffled. The world around him began to dissolve.

Then, the hooker was there, ethereal bosom overflowing her bodice as she unslung Frank's canteen and shoved it to his lips.

As color and life and memory returned, Frank whirled back to the window and snatched up the Winchester. He chambered a round as the boy gained the saddle. He aimed for the spot between the shoulder blades.

The boy turned and looked at him, brown eyes frightened. His Indian nose looked familiar. He was only a boy, not even a man yet. The rifle muzzle dropped a fraction of an inch.

"Shoot, Frank!" Batcho shouted below. "He is a horse thief!"

Frank sighted on the boy's head. No one could fault a man for shooting a horse thief.

"You were a desperate boy once, too," whispered the hooker.

The fog in his mind cleared for an instant, and Frank remembered the thunder of a shotgun, blood spraying, a man's scream.

Cursing, he dropped the rifle. "Hey, kid!" he yelled. "What'll you do with the horse?"

The boy turned see-through, wavering like a mirage. Frank upended the canteen in his mouth, but nothing came out. Beside him, the hooker had nearly disappeared, only a coil of golden hair remaining.

"I'll sell it," the boy yelled back. "We're hungry."

He pointed down the street, where a sickly, thin Indian woman stood, with fierce eyes and a nose like the thief's. That gaze sent cold fingers down Frank's back. The woman had been watching him for years. She knew him better than he knew himself, and the boy was hers.

"Take him," Frank yelled. "Old Man Stevenson will give you good money for him. And there's some jerky and a loaf of bread in the saddle bags."

The boy nodded as they all faded from sight, and Frank stood alone in a cobwebbed room, holding a rusted rifle.

On the street below, Batcho shook his head. "I hope you were right, Frank Butcher."

CHAPTER FIVE

$\mathbf{F}$rank mounted an underworld reincarnation of his old gelding, the one the boy had tried to steal. The horse's frail frame looked too weak to hold Frank's weight, with fur sloughing off and bits of hide dragging on the ground. But its eyes burned red, and it tossed its head as he climbed into a rotted saddle. To Frank's surprise, the horse did not collapse, but kicked at the dirt with one hoof.

"Where's your horse?" Frank asked Batcho.

The Indian shrugged.

"Horses don't like me. I'll keep up, don't worry."

So Frank kicked his decaying mount in the flanks and held on for dear life as it leaped forward faster than any horse he'd ever ridden. Cactus whipped past, rocks nothing more than blurs. To Frank's shock, Batcho did keep up, changing into a coyote that loped along beside him as if it were no effort.

"We should slow down," Batcho-coyote told him. "You will kill your horse."

Frank urged the horse faster. "Seems to me it's already dead. Besides, if time is so crucial, why the

Hell you trying to slow me down?"

The coyote stumbled, regained his stride, but said nothing.

"Thought so," Frank muttered.

Urgency pulled at Frank, a need to move forward. He had to understand. He'd thought all of his kills justified, but now, he wondered. Doubt had chewed its way into his mind like a rat into a sack of grain.

"What are you chasing, Frank Butcher?" asked Batcho as they crossed from desert to plains in a single blurred instant.

"The boy," he answered. "I need to know who he is."

"You may not like what you learn."

"Reckon I won't, but that's never stopped me before."

Batcho said nothing.

Another river wound its way across their path ahead, bending back and forth on itself, like it had nowhere to be anytime soon.

"That the Arkansas ahead?"

"Yes," Batcho answered. "Near—"

"Fort Dodge, Kansas," Frank finished for him. "We're going backward through time."

He knew this kill was no good. He'd known it at the time, but had never been able to admit it until now. He felt no pride at this kill, but he didn't regret it either.

They slowed to a trot, Frank's mount heaving for breath.

Batcho—back to half-man form—opened his mouth to say something, but Frank silenced him with a glare. He listened, and for a moment, Frank heard something. Sorrowful and mourning, the voice reached his ears, then disappeared.

"You should not rush into this," the Indian guide told him. "If you die here—"

"I know, I'm stuck here forever. But if I am late, I'm stuck here too. Nice arrangement your *judges* made."

"You should not mock them. They will spare you no mercy."

"I don't want their mercy. Don't need it, either."

His horse slowed to a walk as the town across the river came into sight.

He heard it again, the same agonized voice. It rose on the wind, carried from the river, strengthening as they neared the banks. Not a single voice, but dozens, even hundreds of voices layered atop one another, all wailing and moaning, crying out in pain and torment.

He looked at Batcho, but his guide shrugged.

The horse stopped a few yards from the water's edge, stomping and snorting, refusing to go any farther. It shook its frightening head, red foam flying, as if trying to drive the haunting sounds from its mind.

Frank hopped down. The closer he got, the louder the wailing became. He covered his ears, but it didn't help. The sound punched through his flesh and embedded itself in his mind like an arrow quivering in a tree.

He could feel the voices eroding his sanity, too. Like wind chiseling at a rock, the noise wore his resolve.

He knelt by the water and reached out his hand.

"No!" Batcho snapped. "It is too powerful. You will lose yourself in their agony forever."

"You said I gotta remember before I relive," Frank told him. "Now, let me do it so I can get out of this place."

He thrust his fist into the water.

Screaming erupted in his mind, a tormenting wail so exquisitely sad that Frank thought of drowning himself in the river. Under the water, faces appeared, mouths open and crying. Yet nothing seemed familiar, and he recognized neither the voices nor the faces.

It wasn't enough. He needed to see, to remember everything. He needed something to connect his mind and soul to this place and this kill. There was only one way.

Without a word, Frank flung himself into the Arkansas.

* * *

Frank pauses, hand halfway to his mouth, a strip of jerky pinched between thumb and forefinger. His right hand strays to the pistol at his hip. To his right, his horse nickers and stomps.

He sits on a rotting log inside a stand of willows, oaks, and maples, the evening sun slicing through the green overhead canopy in dusty orange blades. Across the tiny clearing, a twig snaps. He can't see through the thick underbrush, but he knows the clumsy sound of a man trying too hard to be quiet.

Stuffing the jerky in his mouth, Frank draws his Colt and lies on his back, head resting against the log. He pushes his hat down over his eyes and hides the gun under a flap of his tan duster. Trusting his other senses, he closes his eyes.

A rustle of leaves and footsteps tell him a man has entered the clearing. Frank wants to risk a peek, but knows he cannot, so he waits, finger on the trigger.

The man creeps forward, feet crunching on dried leaves and brittle twigs. A pistol hammer clicks back. A vague shape stops, towering over Frank, blocking the warm sun.

Somewhere to the south, a wolf howls, its cry sending a flock of birds into sudden flight as it rips through the clearing. A second answers, and a third. Frank's horse dances and snorts.

Frank senses motion from the stranger. Without warning, Frank tips his gun up and shoots, rolling away to his feet. The man screams and fires, but misses. Frank opens his eyes and fires again, this time knocking the man to the ground.

Frank moves lightning-fast, kicking the pistol from the man's hand. He stands over him, Colt trained on his forehead.

The other is a lawman with a tarnished U.S.

Marshal's badge beside the bullet hole in his short coat. Frank doesn't recognize him, with his frightened green eyes and ginger beard, sprinkled with salty white. He holds up his hands before him, cringing and looking away. Red froth bubbles between his lips. He looks small and afraid, like a child in the dark. Frank pities him, but not much.

"Please, don't shoot," the marshal begs, his lips trembling. His voice is high-pitched. He wipes at his brow, knocking his hat off to reveal a bald head, peeling with sunburn.

"Tell me why I shouldn't kill you," Frank says.

"I can help you," the marshal says. "You're wanted for murder, Frank. Every lawman between here and Topeka's looking for you." He coughs, a racking, metallic noise that sprays blood down his beard.

"Tell me something I don't know."

"I could get you out of here alive. Tell folks you're my deputy marshal, taking me for care into Fort Dodge. Then, when I'm healed, we could make it all the way to Oklahoma before anyone knew."

If Frank hates anything more than a coward, it's a lying coward.

"I don't need your help. Made it this far on my own."

Beyond the trees, the wolves howl, closer this time. The marshal's eyes open wide.

"Frank, please. I didn't mean anything personal by it. I just needed the reward."

"What's your name, Marshal?" Frank asks.

"John Webber."

"And what's the price on my head these days, Marshal Webber?"

"Two hundred, dead or alive."

"I don't suppose you care which way you deliver me, either."

"Magistrate said he'd pay an extra fifty for dead," he sputters. "I need the money bad. I have—"

The wolves howl again, a sound like human wailing, telling of pain and sorrow, longing, and of course, hunger. The marshal glances toward the trees.

"Worried about the horse you left out there?" Frank asks.

Webber nods.

"Well, don't." Frank moves away, holstering his gun and snatching the marshal's up off the ground. "I'll grab him on my way out. He'll be in good hands."

He picks up his food, stuffs it in his own saddlebag, and stands over the dying marshal.

"Please don't leave me here. They're coming, hungry. I can hear them."

Frank can too—rustling in the trees to their south, from where the howling had come. They smell the marshal's blood.

"Stay real still," he tells the lawman. "Maybe they won't see you."

He swings into the saddle and steers his horse north out of the clearing, the marshal babbling nonsense in his lady-voice.

Outside, Frank finds a bay mare, saddled and waiting, with a Winchester lever action rifle and full saddle bags. He grabs the reins and is about to leave when a lone, single wolf howls inside the clearing. A moment later, the marshal screams.

* * *

Frank swam to the far bank of the Arkansas to find Batcho waiting for him.

"Do you hear it, Frank Butcher?" he asked, shifting from paw to paw.

Frank stood and cupped his hand against his ear. In the distance, he heard them, voices stacked atop one another, carried on the wind. A moment later, the wind died and the voices faded.

"Yeah, I hear 'em. I reckon we ought to get going."

They followed a path through the prairie lands, a thin, dirt track cut through the tall wheat. When the wind blew, the wailing got louder. When it died, the cries died with it.

Before long, the copse of trees came into view, and as if on cue, the wailing jumped up, no longer dependent on wind for legs. The hair on Frank's arms stood up.

"Wait here," Frank told Batcho. "I'll come back for you."

Batcho nodded, and Frank left him. He didn't try to be quiet. He pushed and shoved his way through the underbrush, making more noise than a bowl. It didn't matter—the marshal would be expecting him anyway.

Frank burst into the clearing, shoving a branch from his face, and found the marshal reclined against the log, his hat down over his face, hands crossed over his chest. Frank drew his pistol and took a step.

The marshal must have heard him, for he jerked to his feet, hat flying back off his bald head. Frank almost dropped his gun. The man's mouth gaped like a cavern with pale, sharpened teeth forming a jagged circle around the opening. What came out sounded like the man's soul being ripped from his body. Frank covered his ears, but it did no good — the sound came just as loud, just as agonizing.

Frank raised his gun, but before he could shoot, a wolf stepped into the clearing, carrying a naked human newborn by its neck like it might a cub. The baby looked at Frank, and its mouth opened — a horrifying black portal into death itself — and a cry streamed forth even more terrible than the marshal's. In the baby's cry, Frank heard hunger and sadness, fear and longing.

He dropped to his knees, hands pressed over his ears. Another wolf entered, carrying a toddler whose cries of agony joined the others. Four more wolves came, each carrying a bawling child older than the last, until children from birth to six howled in the clearing. Frank's ears so filled with pain and suffering that he fell face down on the ground, unable to move, body wracked with anguish.

Then Batcho appeared, tugging on Frank's

collar. Frank fought him, wanting to hide his face from the incriminating wails of the marshal's children.

Batcho yelled something at him. Frank could not make out the words, so the Indian leaned closer and screamed into Frank's ear.

"You must shoot him!" he shouted. "The law man. Shoot him and they'll stop."

Frank shook his head. It didn't seem right, but the wailing disrupted his thoughts too much to know why.

"You have to!" Batcho repeated. "Or they will kill you. The marshal was corrupt. He didn't care about you or justice. He wanted the reward money."

The lawman *had* admitted as much the day Frank shot him.

Frank picked up his gun and pointed it at the marshal. The terrible shrieking grew loud enough that his right ear rang and his left trailed warm blood down his neck. He took aim but paused. He had to think like the judges, not a gunfighter.

Of course the marshal wanted—needed even—the reward money. He had six young ones to feed, young ones who'd probably suffered more than they'd deserved following his death. Still, Frank had left the man alive. The wolves had done the killing.

An idea struck him through the din of the wailing.

Frank spun and shot the nearest wolf. The great beast exploded in a shower of crystalline silver, glittering as it cascaded to the ground. The wailing decreased, and the next wolf leapt at him. Frank shot it in mid-air and dove out of the way as its body turned to dust.

A third took Frank's pant leg in its teeth, but Frank shot it between its burning, yellow eyes, and shot a fourth in the side of its chest, both disintegrating into sparkling silver.

Teeth clamped down on his left forearm, shooting fire up into his shoulder as a fifth wolf came out of nowhere. Frank clubbed the animal on the head with his pistol, driving it back, then shot it in the heart. The last wolf—the largest one by far—stalked closer, its fangs dripping blood. The wailing had grown softer now, and Frank corralled his thoughts. Only the youngest child remained, its voice joined with the marshal's to create a cacophony of misery. Frank tracked the last wolf with his gun, one shot remaining. He drew back the hammer, then put himself between the wolf and the marshal.

The wolf stopped, lowered its head a moment, and stared at Frank. Then, it picked up the last baby—the infant—and loped out of the clearing. The marshal vanished.

Frank reloaded his pistol just in case, then took a moment to bandage his forearm before leaving the clearing.

He found Batcho back outside the trees. His horse had galloped off.

"I know where we're going next." He didn't want to think about it, dreaded facing it. "What I don't know is how we're getting there."

For the first time that night, Batcho smiled.

CHAPTER SIX

Frank rested his head against the window of their compartment, letting the frigid cold of the train car's glass ease the pounding in his head. Batcho had changed the bandage on his wounded arm, but Frank still could not feel the fingers on his left hand. Burning lingered in his elbow, and something told him the wound would never fully heal.

He didn't know when it had turned cold outside, but all he saw in the early morning sunlight was ice. Frozen trees stood skeletal against the cemetery-gray of the sky, and the yellow grass of Kansas had given way to frozen stalks of corn sliding past outside the window.

Beside him, Batcho snored, head resting against the wall. Frank wanted to throw the lying red man from the train and let him freeze to death. Yet he needed the Indian—somehow, he would factor large in how this turned out for him. Still, almost everything he'd said was a lie, and Frank knew he could not trust him for sound advice.

He didn't doubt they were on the right train. It had been the only one at the station—a single black passenger car hitched to a gleaming black steam engine, purple smoke belching from its stack. A phantom conductor's voice announced its destination as "Oooomahhhhaaa." It was the right train... that much he knew.

Still, he hated the Indian, wanted to punch him repeatedly on his big, hook nose.

He rubbed his hands together and shook himself. His unreasonable feelings of hatred had to be the effect of the next river, the Missouri. The Colorado had burned, the Rio Grande had made him forget, and the Arkansas had made him hear wailing. The Missouri was making him hate. He couldn't afford to give in to it, or he would spend eternity here.

But he dreaded these next tests. He didn't want to relive either one, to feel their pain all over again. He wondered if his father had felt the same during his testing, and for a moment, guilt gnawed on the bones of his soul.

Then, the brakes clamped with a cold, metallic squeal, and the train slowed. Low buildings—some with lights on, others dark—passed by his window. Ice glazed the glass, making the world outside fuzzy, but men and women shuffled along the streets, blurry shadows like they always were here. The train moved through Omaha, Frank's feet tapping. This was his righteous kill, the one even the judges could not question. The other remaining kill had haunted him his whole life, stalking through his dreams unlike any of the others. He didn't want to relive either, but at least he knew this one had been justified.

As they pulled into the Union Pacific Depot at Tenth Street, Frank dealt the Indian a smack to the head to wake him. Batcho sat up, sputtering, and Frank stood to avoid the urge to hit him again. Damned river. Damned Indian.

But the train didn't stop. It rolled through the depot, crossed the short bridge at Seventh Street, and left the city to the east. The car bucked a bit as it moved out onto the rickety bridge crossing the Missouri. Through the iced-over window, Frank noted the fat, silver line of the river worming its way north. Judging from the color, the river had frozen solid.

The train stopped on the bridge.

"I think we get off here," Batcho said.

Frank followed the red man from the compartment, swallowing the urge to kick him in the back. He focused on the test.

They stepped out onto the ice-slicked bridge, their breath freezing in the cold air. Frank stomped to keep blood moving in his toes and flipped up the collar of his duster.

The cold felt unnatural, more than a normal winter chill. It ate through his coat and clothes, biting deep into his bones and frosting his heart. As they stood at the bridge rail staring out across the gleaming frozen surface of the Missouri, Frank tasted hate's bitter flavor on his tongue.

Hate he understood — knew it like an old friend

renting a room in his soul. He'd felt its shadow growing in him since Fort Dodge, and recognized it now as the source of the cold.

Frank had frozen Omaha himself. And Omaha had frozen him.

He sensed movement behind him and spun, drawing his six shooter. The driver floated behind him, inches off the bridge, black duster billowing in the cold breeze. No breath fogged before his face, but his eyes burned under the brim of his hat.

"I'll do this myself," Frank told him. He stuffed the pistol back in his holster and turned to Batcho. "How thick you reckon that ice is?"

"No way to know."

Frank nodded. He knew what had to come next, feared it would consume him as it almost had in life.

Something appeared under the ice. A face, cold and gray, stared up at him through the glaze. Long, dark hair billowed around it, flushed by the river's current. Frank watched as the face moved downstream, almost directly under the bridge now. He knew that face.

"You know what you must do," Batcho told him.

Frank nodded, and shot a withering glare over his shoulder at the looming shadow of the driver. Then, he took a deep breath and jumped.

The ice broke when he hit, and the frigid waters of the Missouri swallowed him whole. He clamped his hand over his mouth and nose, forcing himself not to breathe as the shock of the water hit him. His legs and arms went numb, and he found himself unable to kick back toward the hole in the ice. As he watched, paralyzed with cold, the hole resealed itself like it had never broken.

Panic rose in his belly. He needed air, but couldn't swim to the surface, his arms and legs unwilling to move. He sank farther from the ice, the dark waters closing in around him.

A hand grasped his collar, tugged him upward, and spun him around. He came face-to-face with the woman he'd seen through the ice. Dead black eyes glared at him as her midnight hair billowed in the water. Her hook nose sat crooked on her face. Frank's heart thudded in his chest; his mind galloped. He would die here in the frozen Missouri and spend the rest of eternity reliving his sins.

The woman pulled him close, her cold, blue lips opening to reveal shattered teeth. He tried to fight, tried to push her away, but couldn't move. She pressed her frozen mouth to his, her swollen tongue forcing his lips apart, and breathed into him. As her breath filled his lungs, everything else around him faded from sight.

* * *

Frank guides his gelding down the long, dirt lane that leads to the white farm house he shares with his wife. He'd never thought he'd marry an Indian, but he'd gotten drunk enough to get her pregnant. Marriage had been the honorable thing to do. She'd lost that baby—and two more since—but he stays with her. She possesses a fierce, hawk-nosed beauty, with dark, tilted eyes, and skin the color of a worn penny. Her silky, midnight hair falls to her waist. Gone two weeks now, he misses touching that hair and is returning a week early out of longing for her.

Her name in Sioux is something he cannot pronounce, so he calls her Lisa.

He reins in and stops. A buggy sits by the front steps, shaded under a willow. He's never seen it before, with its black canopy and dappled mare. Suspicion gnaws at his mind. He has no reason to doubt Lisa's fidelity, but he makes that jump without hesitation. History, he knows, repeats itself.

He hitches his horse to the tree and examines the wagon. Leather, cushioned seats. Expensive whip. Horse groomed to immaculate perfection, its coat glistening with a slight sheen of sweat.

Her visitor hasn't been there long.

Frank tiptoes up the front step, finding the front door open. He slips inside. A man's bowler hangs on the peg by the door, the peg where Frank's hat should hang. A long, black coat drapes over the back of the sitting room chair, the one Frank uses for his morning coffee in the long, cold winter months.

Rage burns in his gut, building from a small, guttering candle to a roaring blaze that threatens to consume him.

A woman giggles upstairs. The low thrum of a

man's voice tumbles down the steps.

Frank mounts the stairs, careful to avoid the creaky third one, and climbs to the top. He pauses, listening, and hears rustling from the main bedroom.

He edges down the hallway, sidling against the wall, until he is outside the door. At first he hears nothing, then his wife lets out a deep moan.

Squaring up, Frank kicks in the door.

His wife lies on the bed, her dress hitched up to her knees. A startled man with a handlebar moustache, sleeves of his white shirt rolled up, looks out from under her petticoats.

Frank draws, even as his wife screams, and the man scampers back against the wall, hands coming up in front of him.

"I assure you, sir, this is not—"

Frank shoots him in the chest, the powerful forty-five knocking the man back against the wall, blood spattering the patterned wallpaper.

Lisa cries out, jumping to her feet. She runs for the man, but Frank catches her by the elbow and spins her to face him.

"You shame me, woman!"

"No, I—"

His backhanded blow hits her so fast, she can't even block it. His knuckles shatter teeth, snapping her head back and to the side. She staggers, but Frank isn't done, his hatred not sated. He snatches her by the hair and flings her against a wall. She hits with a thud and slides to the floor, motionless.

Behind him, the adulterer stirs, rises to one knee, breath wheezing in and out, blood gurgling on his chest. Frank aims the Colt at him and advances, slowly.

"You come into my house and seduce my wife!" he shouts. "There's a special place in Hell for adulterers like you, mister!"

The man lifts one hand, his moustache moving as he tries to form words.

"It's n-not what it s-seems," he sputters. "You must be careful. Lisa, she—"

"Oh, she'll get hers, too," Frank shouts. "She won't get away with cheating on me."

"But I'm—"

Frank shoots him in the head, knocking him backward. He falls still, spots of red mingled with chunks of gray on the wall behind him.

Lisa moans, and Frank goes to her. He lifts her by the arm and punches her, knocking her back to the floor while blood gushes from her misshapen nose. He stands over her, fists bunched at his sides. Hate freezes his heart, puts out the fire of rage that had burned there an instant before. Calm descends over him.

"I'm going to town," he growls. "You'll have your cheating ass out of my house by sundown. If you're here when I get back, I'll kill you like I did him."

She opens her mouth to speak, but he cuts her off.

"I've seen your kind before. You'll rot in Hell for

this."

He storms from the room, crashing down the steps, and slams the door on his way. He mounts his horse and ventures a glance at the bedroom window. Lisa stands there, broken nose somehow still proud, rubbing her belly.

He kicks his horse into a gallop.

* * *

Batcho pulled him quaking from the icy waters, wrapped him in a thick wool blanket, and led him to a fire on the Iowa bank. Frank huddled close to the flames, letting their warmth lick at his face and hands. He couldn't stop shaking, the muscles in his neck bunching with every tremor until his entire head screamed with pain.

"This is the righteous kill," he told Batcho, as the Indian made stew in a cast iron pot. "There's no way I was wrong this time."

He no longer feared reliving that day. It had taken so much out of him the first time that it couldn't possibly take more.

"I believe you," Batcho assured, "but only the opinions of the judges matter."

Frank shook his head. This had to be the one.

They wolfed down the stew, and by the time they were done, Frank's clothes had somehow dried. His shivering had stopped, and he no longer felt frozen to the core.

"Time to go," Batcho said, his tail sweeping side to side in slow arcs. "We must walk to your house."

"I know the way," Frank said, stepping off. "No need for you to go."

The Indian shrugged. "The judges would be quite cross with me if I let you go alone."

Frank bit his tongue to keep his hatred in check, but his right hand unconsciously reached for his pistol. He stopped just short of the handle. "Well, we don't want angry judges, do we?"

Frank's house sat a few miles south of Council Bluffs. Through some memory of their own, his legs carried him while his mind milled around the thoughts colliding in his head. This was his righteous kill. He had to do everything the same, but something nagged at him, whispered that it might not be so. Things here were never as they seemed.

The day stayed clear and deathly cold. Had his clothing not dried so fast, he likely would have frozen. Their breath crystallized before them, and even with his hands in his pockets, his fingertips were numb by the time the old willow tree came into view.

Encased in ice, the willow's branches sparkled in the afternoon sun, stiff and brittle. The house stood behind, icicles as long as his legs hanging from the corners of the roof, frost coating every window.

He tried to breathe deep, but the frigid air turned it into a dry cough. Again, he shivered so hard, his neck and shoulders ached.

"This is it," Batcho said. "You know you are

right. We both know why this man deserved to die. What he took from you."

Frank whirled and grabbed the Indian by the neck with his cold, numb hands. They held more strength than he would have guessed.

"You know nothing about this!" Frank growled, his face just an inch from the Indian's. "So, keep your trap shut, or I might decide my next righteous kill is you."

"I am not the one you hate, Frank Butcher," the Indian said, his voice calm. "Killing me will bring you only eternal suffering. The man you hate is inside the house. Touching your wife. Remember her moans?"

Frank's grip tightened on the guide's throat, making his brown eyes bulge. But Batcho was right. The target of Frank's hatred was inside the house.

Frank released the Indian, noting with satisfaction the finger marks on his neck, then turned to face the house. Steeling himself, he went inside, eager for blood. Inside, he marched up the stairs and kicked in the bedroom door.

Lisa lay on the bed, frozen stiff and covered in ice, the man with the moustache kneeling between her open legs. Neither of them moved even a hair when he entered.

This was his chance. He moved to the kneeling man's side, drew his gun, and pulled back the hammer. But again, something whispered in his mind that all was not right. He hesitated and looked around, trying to find what troubled him. The man's sleeves were rolled up, but his clothing remained on. A pile of clean, white sheets lay on the floor beside the bed.

His wife moved, the ice around her cracking and popping. Frank stepped back, his gun dropping to his side. The ice shattered, fragments flying and peppering Frank's body like buckshot. His wife stood on the bed, black hair sticking out in all directions, as frozen as the willow outside. Her skin had turned a ghastly blue, and her breath clouded in ice crystals as she hissed it out. Frost glittered on her lashes as her eyes—now pale blue instead of brown—focused on her husband.

She hissed, showing icicle fangs. Beside Frank, the other man unfroze, rising to his feet.

"She mustn't," he said. "Too dangerous."

Frank focused on his wife. She stalked forward, bed springs creaking, and reached out her skeletal hand. Her fingernails raked at him, forcing him back another two steps. Her next swipe came fast from her other hand, almost too quick for him to dodge. He rolled to his left, pistol coming up. He didn't fire. Why were the man's clothes still on?

Lisa leapt for him, her ice-claws slashing the air. He dove right, coming to his feet by the bed. A satchel sat on the floor by the post, black leather, buckled on top. Lisa landed on the floor and crouched in a corner.

"No, no, she must be still," said the man. "This won't do at all."

Frank risked a glance down at the bag. A single

tag had been sewn into the dark leather. It read, "Dr. George Martin, OB."

What kind of doctor was an OB? So many different kinds of doctors were coming out these days, they were impossible to keep straight.

"He was a doctor?" he asked, looking into his wife's frozen eyes.

She snarled at him, but did not move.

"Were you sick?"

She inched forward, jaw snapping.

"All right, not sick," he said. "He was looking at you down there. Were you—"

He dropped to his knees, sudden grief chilling him to his core.

"Oh, God," escaped his lips.

She leapt at him, pouncing cat-like, ice flaking from her body as she landed in front of him. Frank jumped across the bed to the window. She glared at him, creeping up onto the bed, her icicle fingers shredding the sheets.

"You *must* stay calm!" the doctor shouted, his eyes vacant and staring ahead. "For the baby, you must not over exert!"

She ignored him, jumping off the bed, driving Frank against the window. A tiny bulge at her belly told him he was right—she was carrying his child. Had been when he'd—

She swatted at him, one ice cold nail tearing into his cheek, the trickle of blood the only warmth in the room. Frank winced.

"Lisa, I'm sorry," he begged. "I didn't know."

She swung again, but this time, he dodged it. He tried the window, but ice held it closed. Left with no choice, he drew his gun.

Lisa stalked closer, her fangs dripping ice, wiry limbs blue. She was going to kill him if he let her. But if he shot her, he'd spend eternity seeing her this way...knowing what he'd done.

She raised her hands, ready to slash his throat. Frank wheeled, shot out the window, and dove through.

CHAPTER SEVEN

Water sprayed Frank's face from the paddle wheel at the rear of the riverboat *Lypi*. They steamed south along the Mississippi, he and Batcho the only two passengers aboard besides the driver who now manned the wheel of the boat. Like the other four rivers, the Mississippi flowed the wrong direction, north and west, making the boat fight against the current while paddling southward. Frank wondered how long he'd been fighting against the current himself. He had a feeling he was about to find out.

So far, all four of his kills were injustices caused by his misperception of the events around him. His own failings. His fault.

That meant...but no, that was impossible. The judges were wrong, plain and simple.

Dark clouds scudded across the sky as the *Lypi* approached a bend in the river. Around that bend lay Vicksburg, Mississippi, Frank's childhood home.

Lightning streaked from cloud to cloud, chased by a low roll of thunder. The wind picked up, making Frank hold his hat on his head with one hand.

A splash of water hit his face, making him wince. Everywhere a droplet struck his skin, pain flared as if the drops had turned to stones. Or bullets. He turned away, wiping his face on his sleeve. Batcho looked at him, eyebrows arching.

"Are you well, Frank Butcher?"

Frank nodded as hard pellets of water struck the back of his neck. He moved out of the paddle's spray. Lightning flashed and thunder tore through the air, closer now.

"I'm trying to think why my guide, who's supposed to help me, would lie to me every step of the way."

"What are you talking about?" Batcho asked, stepping back. He slipped on the wet planks, his coyote toenails clawing for traction.

"You know damn well what I'm talking about, Batcho," Frank snapped. He winced as the boat splashed through a wave, sending a buckshot spray of water across his back. "You've mislead me on every test. You've pushed me where you wanted me to go, not where I needed to be. If I'd listened to you, I'd already be condemned to this underworld forever."

He stepped toward the Indian, fists clenched. Batcho clattered back a few uneasy steps, scraggly tail drooping.

"I give you advice, Frank Butcher. I do not know how the judges want you to act."

"Horse crap! That middle judge wants to see me in Hell. You've been helping him by pointing me toward the wrong move at every stop. I'm tempted to teach you a lesson right here and now."

The boat turned hard to the right, sending Batcho sliding toward him. Frank tried to dodge, but his boots slipped on the wet deck, and the Indian took him out at the knees. They slid, tangled, against the rail. Frank's hat blew into the river.

Water sprayed from the wheel, drenching them. Frank arched his back and grunted as a convulsing pain ripped through his chest and arms. He managed to roll away, but not before an image flashed in his mind.

The silhouette of a man, dark and foreboding, stands with fists clenched over a woman crumpled on the ground before him.

"No, not this!" Frank cried, shaking his head. The boat pitched again, and more water washed over him, biting deeper this time, lancing through muscle and bone to his heart. He grasped at his chest as another image invaded his mind.

The woman cowers, bloody and bruised, her hands raised in front of her face.

"Get out of my head!" Frank yelled. He gained his feet and rushed the Indian, driving him back against the rail. "Make it stop! I know what I did!"

Batcho struggled free of Frank's grip, the water making him slippery. He tried to dance out of reach, but fell to the deck with a grunt, his coyote paws kicking.

"This isn't the answer," Batcho shouted, his hands up in defense. "You need to pass this test. It will be the hardest on you, but you must."

"I'll kill you!" Frank gripped the rail and levered himself to his feet. "Then, this will all go away."

"Killing me will strand you here, Frank Butcher. You must face this, whatever it is. This is your last test."

A bolt of lightning struck the far shore, splitting an oak tree down the middle. Wind howled around them, and Batcho slid on the wet deck planks.

Frank looked over his shoulder as Vicksburg came into sight on the eastern shore. Row upon row of low buildings huddled under the approaching storm. Smoke slithered up from some, swallowed by the wall of billowing clouds. Behind the little city, a curtain of rain bore down, gray as death.

Batcho managed to clatter toward Frank, leaning into the wind.

"Let me help you," he called. "I can—"

"No!" Frank shouted. "You've done enough damage. This is too much. I can't—"

A gust of wind blew paddle spray across his back, the pain of a hundred nails piercing his flesh.

The dark man approaches, his fist drawn back.

"No!" Frank clawed at his face, trying to rip the images from his mind.

Another gust, more water, searing pain.

The woman screams. A shotgun booms. Blood sprays.

"Make it stop!" Frank charged the Indian, intent on ripping his throat out.

But Batcho regained his footing, stepped to the

side, and moved against the rail where Frank had been. Frank skidded to a stop and wheeled.

"Do not do this, Frank Butcher!"

So much blood, he thinks he will drown in it. The woman's sobs pierce his ear drums.

Frank rushed, reaching for the Indian's neck, his hands claw-like before him. Batcho stepped aside again, grabbing Frank's wrist and throwing him against the rail. The boat pitched down and the wind reversed, buffeting Frank in the chest. He teetered on the rail, and fell.

The water felt like stone when he hit, pain exploding through his body, his bones feeling like they would snap. Water filled his ears and nose, making his head scream, and a million points of iron seemed to pierce his skin.

He fought to stay conscious, knowing where he would end up if he didn't. He couldn't go there. He wasn't ready. But the pain, the crushing, squeezing, pulverizing pain overwhelmed his body, and before he could stop it, he went back to the first time he killed.

* * *

Frank guides the wagon down the rutted dirt path toward their home, his father snoring in the back with their sacks of grain and boxes of supplies. Frank catches a whiff of the whiskey, something that's surrounded his father for all Frank's fourteen years. It's familiar, like the smell of manure or his mother's hair. Almost comforting. Almost.

The house comes into view around a bend, white clapboard shining in the setting sun, windows dark. Frank reins in, the wagon lurching to a stop. The sudden halt wakes his father. Jim Butcher sits up, rubs his eyes.

"What'd ya stop for?"

"Someone's at the house," Frank tells him. "Horse out front."

His father squints. The sun sets behind them, over Vicksburg, some two days ride from here, but the raking orange light is enough for his father to see the horse tethered under a huge, towering oak tree.

"Damn it," Jim says, snatching up the double-barrel shotgun from the wagon bed. "I told that nigger boy never to come around here. And I told your mother to keep him away. Move it now!"

Frank snaps the reins, the horse taking off at a trot. The whiskey smell comes stronger to him now, staler, and it mingles with the scent of his father's rage.

Frank's hands tremble on the reins.

They skid to a stop out front, making the other horse jump and whinny. It can smell his father's anger, and wants to run. Animals know things before they happen, and this one senses death coming.

Frank's mother bursts out the door, her flaming red hair tumbled from its normal tight bun. She nearly falls down the porch steps trying to reach her enraged husband, catching herself on the railing.

Her bare feet kick up dust behind her.

"Jim, don't hurt him!" she pleads.

His father jumps down, the shotgun in his hands. She puts her hands on his chest, her eyes begging through cascades of tears.

Jim backhands her, a sweeping, upward blow that snaps her head back and sends her sprawling in the dirt. Frank tenses, resisting the urge to help his mother — it will make things worse. He's learned over the years.

A black man stumbles from the front door, his hat in his hand. He wears denim overalls, his white shirt unbuttoned nearly to his belly, suspenders down at his sides. His skin is the darkest black Frank has ever seen, his eyes and teeth snowy white against it. His nose fans out on his face like a river delta.

He sees Frank's mother on the ground. He snarls and rushes Jim Butcher.

The shotgun roars and the black man flies backward, blood blossoming in the air around him. He hits the ground with a sickening crunch.

Frank's mother screams, hysterical now, and climbs to her feet. Her husband slaps her hard across the cheek, putting her back in the dirt, then stomps over to the dying black man.

Frank looks away as the shotgun roars again.

His father marches back to where Frank's mother lays dazed in the dirt. He tosses the shotgun on the ground and drags her to her feet.

"I'm not man enough for you?" he shouts, his

face a ghoulish shadow of its normal appearance. "You need some nigger between your legs to feel pretty?"

His mother's eyes flash, and she squares her shoulders as much she can in her husband's harsh grip.

"You're never here! And even when you are, you've got no time for me. What do you care, anyway?"

He grabs her by the neck and shakes, her head snapping from side-to-side with disgusting cracking sounds. Frank covers his ears, but cannot make himself look away. His father pulls back his fist and punches her. She crumples to the ground in a heap.

Tears burn in Frank's eyes. His mother's beautiful hair splays out in the dirt, like melting copper, and blood gushes from her broken nose. His father stands over her, leans down, and slaps her until she wakes up. Then, he grabs the collar of her dress and pulls her face close to his.

"There's a special place in Hell for adulterers like you," he snarls.

He shoves her back down and looks at Frank. "Son, reload that shotgun and bring it here."

Frank hesitates until his father straightens and takes a step toward him, face darkening. Frank's seen that look before and knows what will befall him if he doesn't obey. He grabs two shotgun cartridges from the box in the wagon and jumps down, knees screaming with the sudden jolt. His hands shake as he breaches the shotgun, and he struggles to jam the shells into their chambers.

"Done yet?" his father yells. He's sitting on Frank's mother's chest, his right hand pressing on her throat. He holds out the left hand for the shotgun. "Give it here, and I'll show you what you do to a cheatin' whore like her."

Frank's mother looks at him, her right eye swollen shut, and smiles. She gives him the slightest of nods. She knows what will happen to her if Frank obeys, but prefers it over what will happen to Frank if he does not.

Frank rises and walks toward his father, the shotgun pointed down. He never takes his eyes off his mother. Part of him longs to run to her, to fall into her arms and make all the anger and hatred and pain disappear. Another part of him roils at the image of the black man's huge lips on her mouth, of his dark-as-night body against hers. That part of him wants to kick her while she's down, to scream at her for destroying their family. That part of him hates her like his father does.

The little boy in him battles with the man. The boy loves his mama. His world revolves around her. The man rages against her, wants her punished, as if it will stop his own pain.

Frank pauses a few feet away, eyes locked on his mother. She nods again, a movement his father overlooks or doesn't see. Frank makes up his mind and hefts the shotgun across his chest.

"Get off her," he says.

His father's eyes narrow, then his face twists.

"What did you say, boy?"

Frank looks his father in the eye and pulls back the hammer on the right barrel. "I said get off her."

His father stands, swaying. He points at his son. "You'll regret this, boy. I'm your father, and I'll—"

"Step back now." Frank raises the shotgun in his father's direction. "I don't wanna shoot you by mistake."

Confusion flutters across his father's face as the whiskey slows his understanding. Then, he smiles and steps back.

"Gonna do it yourself, eh?" he said, nodding. "That's my boy. Like father like son, I always say."

Frank moves to his mother's side, the shotgun aimed at her head. "Daddy's right. You sinned with that black man. I saw you once before, when Daddy was gone. I watched you through a hole in the wall. You're a whore."

His mother's eyes well, her lip trembles. "I'm sorry, baby," she says. "I never meant…"

Her voice trails off into sobs.

Frank looks at his father, standing to his right. His father nods, a satisfied grin on his face, cruelty dancing in his eyes.

"But you're still my mama," Frank whispers.

He whirls, gun coming up, and fires. His father's left shoulder rocks back, his arm snapping grotesquely, then falling to the ground. Frank staggers back a step, but doesn't fall. His father drops to his knees, eyes wide, staring at the bloody stump where his left arm had been. He screams, even as his right hand fumbles for the six-gun at his side.

"You ain't no son of mine! You'll join your mama in Hell!"

Tears streaming down his cheeks, Frank points the shotgun at his father's chest and fires again.

* * *

Frank sobbed, curled on the lush, green bank of the Mississippi, his knees up to his chest. He heard Batcho's voice as if the Indian guide stood a mile away instead of right next to him. Part of him knew he should listen, should get up and get moving, but that part of him had shrunk into the deep recesses of his mind, buried by tons of grief and despair.

He'd killed his father. That stood in condemnation of his soul, no matter the results of these tests. He'd shot the man who'd raised him, taught him to shoot, to hunt, to ride, rope, and fight. He'd gunned him down to protect a whore, a woman who'd cheated, who'd destroyed their family. He'd chosen sides in the long war between his parents, and now, he feared he'd chosen wrong.

Even worse, he'd let that killing warp him, turn him into something his mother would have found appalling. How many times since that day had he chosen wrong? Had he ever really been righteous again?

By choosing to help one, he'd failed them both. Failed himself.

"Frank Butcher, we must go."

The Indian touched his shoulder with feather-light fingers. Frank brushed them away.

"I don't need to face the judges. I have my answer."

"You misunderstand," Batcho explained. His voice was soft and warm as a blanket. "You cannot learn the truth from memories. They are but fragments of the truth, not all of it. Your truth comes next, during the last test. If you choose well, you will leave this place and forget forever the pain it has brought you."

"I can't shoot him again," Frank said. "No matter what he does. He was my father."

"Maybe you won't have to," Batcho replied with a shrug. "At least the test gives you a chance to make things right."

Frank sighed, climbed to his feet, and pushed past the Indian. "I know the way."

He started east, reached a dirt road, and turned south.

The house lay southeast of town, in the middle of a never-ending cornfield. The stalks stood eight feet high, making a dark corridor of the path leading to the house, ears the size of his forearm everywhere.

When they reached the house, he caught his breath. Like the corn stalks, the house had swollen to twice its normal size. Each step leading to the porch was two feet tall, the roof at least forty feet high. The solid maple door stood fourteen feet tall, and the windows arched just as high.

Before it, Frank felt tiny and afraid. Insignificant.

Hitched out front was the black man's horse, no larger than it had been in life. It tossed its chestnut head at their approach.

"What now?" Batcho asked.

"We wait," Frank said.

A moment later, footsteps sounded behind them. Frank pulled Batcho behind the oak tree. When his father turned the corner onto the path, Frank nearly ran away. It took every nugget of courage he could muster to stand behind the tree and watch the larger-than-life version of his father thunder down the path. At least twelve feet tall, Jim Butcher rippled with muscle he hadn't possessed in life, once-thin shoulders now broad and hewn, arms chiseled. His forehead hung lower over his eyes than Frank remembered, but the cruelty in those eyes remained. In his right hand, he held the old double-barrel shotgun, little more than a pistol for him.

The giant stopped, saw the horse.

"Nigger!" he roared. The horse whinnied, tore free from its hitch, and took off at a terrified gallop.

Frank winced. His father's voice hurt like an ice pick driven in behind his eyes. Jim Butcher's giant stomped past and stood in front of the house.

The giant Jim looked ready to bellow something else when the front door opened, and Frank's mother ran out. She wasn't a giant like her husband, standing five-foot-two like she had in life. She rushed at her husband, throwing her arms around his waist, her face buried in his stomach.

Jim tossed her to the ground like a child's discarded doll, her body hitting the rock-hard dirt with a thump. Frank twisted and writhed, as he felt the pain of his mother's impact, the bruising of her flesh.

The black man came out the door next, his ebony skin gleaming in the sunlight. He hadn't grown, either. His pearly white eyes darted about in fear as he looked at Frank's mother on the ground, then at Jim Butcher, then back again.

Without a word, the black man turned and ran away.

Cold and calculating, Jim Butcher aimed the shotgun one-handed and shot the negro in the back. Blood sprayed from a fist-sized hole, and the man landed face-down in the dirt. Frank's mother tried to run to him, but Jim Butcher backhanded her, sending her flying. She landed in the dirt a few feet from the tree, the pain wracking Frank's body, dropping him to his knees. His mother lay still in the dirt, the subtle rise and fall of her chest all that told him she lived. As Frank's pain eased, he managed to stand.

Jim Butcher stood over the unmoving form of the black man, took careful aim with the shotgun, and blew his head into what looked like a pumpkin dropped from a rooftop.

Frank ducked back behind the tree as his father stormed over to tower above his unconscious mother.

"Frank!" his giant-father bellowed. The words echoed in Frank's head, hitting like a fist. "Franklin D. Butcher, you get your cowardly little hide out here right this minute!"

Frank found himself stepping from behind the tree, hands trembling. His whole body felt battered and bruised, like all his bones were straining not to break.

"There you are, boy." Jim threw the shotgun into the dirt at his feet. "Go reload this and bring it back to me. I'll show you the right way to deal with a lying, cheating, nigger-loving whore of a woman."

Frank hesitated. He wasn't a little boy any more. His father was long dead. He couldn't order him around.

"Move boy, now!"

Frank's head rocked back like he'd been hit, and he felt his lower lip swell, tasted the salty iron of blood in his mouth. He jumped, and before he knew it, he was at the wagon, pushing cartridges into the breach of each barrel.

As he snapped the shotgun closed, a fierce pressure squeezed his head, like someone was trying to crush it. Jim had lifted his mother by the head, holding her even with his face.

Frank took one step before giant-Jim shook his mother, sending Frank into a spasm of pain. His body jerked and convulsed like his mother's, and when Jim tossed her motionless body to the ground, Frank fell, too.

"Hurry up, boy!" Jim shouted.

Then, he looked and saw his son lying in the dirt, crumpled and hurting, and his features softened. For an instant, the cruelty left his eyes, and he seemed to shrink a little.

"Frank, you all right, son?" This time, the voice didn't hurt, but soothed Frank's aches and pains, relieved the pressure in his head. "Are you hurt?"

Frank used the shotgun like a crutch and pushed to his feet. He shook his head.

"Well, son, bring me the gun, then." His father had shrunk to almost normal size now, his shoulders thin, arms wiry.

Frank hesitated, then shook his head.

Jim Butcher straightened himself. "Do as I tell you, boy. Now."

The words pushed Frank, poking and prodding, reminding the son his father could hurt him if he chose.

"She's had enough," Frank managed the courage to say. "You taught her good. Now, leave her be so she can live in shame."

"Don't you tell me what to do, boy!" Jim's shoulders bulged, his words punching Frank in the gut, doubling him over. He grew tall again, his brow lowering, the cold cruelty back in his eyes. "There's a special place in Hell for adulterers, and I'm sending her there."

Frank went down on one knee, his body clenched in pain. His right eye swelled almost shut.

"I...won't...let you," he breathed between gasps

of pain.

His father tilted his head back and roared, the sound knocking Frank on his back. He heard a rib pop, felt fire burning in his lungs. The shotgun skittered out of his grasp.

"You whore-loving little coward!" Jim stomped toward him now, hands reaching. Frank fought back the pounding in his head, spit out a tooth, and grabbed the shotgun. He aimed it at his father's chest.

"Don't make me do it!" the words tumbled out with sobs and drops of blood. "Please!"

His father kept coming, ham-sized fists clenched. "Do it, you little shit! Do it, and I'll haunt you the rest of eternity!"

"You already do!" Frank screamed. And he pulled the trigger.

The shotgun blew a hole right through his father's chest, the pale blue of the Mississippi sky shimmering in the vacant space. Jim Butcher looked down, his features soft, eyes pained. "You…killed me."

Frank said nothing, unable to speak over the pummeling of his own sobs. Closing his eyes, he fired the second barrel at his father's face.

CHAPTER EIGHT

Frank slumped in his seat at the front of the Tombstone courtroom, staring at his hands on the hard, wooden table before him. He tried not to look around, tried not to think about the skeletal bodies hanging from the gallows outside. He knew if he looked right or left, he'd see the eerie, moving pictures of those condemned by the court. They were portals, Batcho had told him, showing the eternal suffering of those the court found unrepentant. Set against the bleached white plaster of the courtroom walls, they had frightened Frank almost to the point of throwing up. One behind the bench had been draped in black cloth. Batcho told him it was too terrible for anyone to look upon.

So Frank stared at his own hands, surprised they did not shake.

A ghostly voice at the head of the room spoke, echoing off the high, beamed ceiling. "All rise!"

Frank stood. The voice came from a bailiff, a stout figure with a sheriff's badge on his tattered vest, twin six guns around his waist, and the horns of a bull erupting from his temples.

"Remain standing for the entrance of their honors, the judges presiding over this court of the underworld."

The judges entered and Frank wanted to run from the room. Eternity facing his sins—even murdering his father over and over—might be better than facing these three. As huge as they'd been in Yuma, they were even more frightening here, where the light made them clearer.

All three wore black robes, and seemed to ooze into the room, like oil stains spreading across the rotting wood floors. The first had a pale, round face, a short bushy moustache of black, with jowls jiggling low and blue eyes that pierced Frank's skull like they were reading his mind. A black bowler sat straight on his head.

The third was thinner and taller, with a moustache so long, it nearly touched his collar bones under slit-like eyes of a cold, hard green. His skin was paler than the first, almost gray in its pallor, and his black hat perched crooked on his head.

The middle one came cloaked in shadow top to bottom, a great billowing hood hiding his face. Frank caught a glimpse of a stubbly beard, but nothing more. No mouth, no nose. Two blazing red eyes, baleful and terrifying. Frank shivered.

The judges didn't sit, nor did they order anyone else to do so. The middle judge picked up a gavel and rapped on the bench, a sound like a coffin being nailed shut.

"Frank Butcher, we'll keep this proceeding short." His voice sounded like granite sliding on gravel. "As a gunfighter, you've killed many times, four of them unjust. You requested trial by testing to clear your name, and have completed all five tests without breaking our rules or dying, meaning you will leave this place. We will now pass judgment on the nature of your heart and announce your sentence. Do you have anything to say before we begin?"

"I didn't want to kill him," Frank said. He lacked the energy to stand, so he dropped to his chair. "I was just a boy. I know I did wrong. I should have found a way…"

He lost his will to speak, letting the sentence trail off.

"My client rests his opening statement, your honors," Batcho said for him. "We await your judgment."

Frank wanted nothing more than to have it over with. He knew the outcome already. He'd killed his own father. He was guilty, an evil man with an evil heart. He deserved Hell.

The judges spoke as one this time, their voices reaching out from the grave, cold and dead.

"In the matter of the death of David Caldwell, killed near Yuma for cheating at cards, we find you wrongly killed this man, but cleared your heart through testing. Caldwell had a sick wife to care for, and in testing, you forgave his cheating and spared his life, demonstrating compassion you did not show while living."

Frank said nothing. He didn't care.

"In the matter of the death of Ronald Butcher in Albuquerque for attempted horse theft—"

Franklin vaulted to his feet. "What was his name?"

Batcho cleared his throat and leaned close. "My apologies, your honors, my client did not mean—"

"Ronald Butcher," the judges answered, their voices cold, emotionless. "Your son."

Frank dropped back into his chair, the breath leaving his body in a whoosh. His son. He remembered the hook nose and the half-Indian skin. The fierce eyes. He should have recognized his own boy. Should have known the shell of his wife standing watch over him.

"What have I done?" Frank whispered.

"The defendant will rise!" the bailiff hissed.

Batcho pulled Frank to his feet, but the gunfighter slumped in his grasp. First his father, then his son. He'd killed his past and his future.

"You wrongly killed your own son," the judges went on, "but cleared yourself in testing, sparing the boy's life without knowing he was yours so that he might help his mother."

Frank hardly heard the words as he swallowed the bitter taste of guilt and despair.

"In the matter of the death of Marshall John Webber, we find you did wrongfully kill a righteous lawman, robbing his children of love and support. But you cleared your heart through testing by saving his life. This vote, however, was not unanimous."

Frank looked up to see the middle judge's red eyes burning hotter than ever.

"In the matter of the death of Doctor George Martin, we find you did wrongfully kill the man while he tried to ensure your son was born healthy. We further find you wrongly and cruelly brutalized your wife during this murder."

A tear ran down Frank's cheek, stinging in the still healing slice on his right cheek. A son. He'd had a son. Images of the dead boy floated in the air before him, mingled with those of his father. The same inky black cloud that had engulfed the OK Corral swirled around them.

"However, we find that during testing, and due to extenuating emotional circumstances, you cleared your heart of malice."

Frank looked up. If those four kills were unjust, that meant—

"Finally, in the matter of the death of James Butcher, your father, we find you did rightfully and justifiably shoot him in self-defense and defense of your mother, brutally beaten until she sought solace in the arms of another man. Further, we find that this justifiable homicide did create mitigating circumstances, causing a life of violence and the unjustified killings of four people, including your son."

Frank stared at the judges, mouth open.

The middle judge drew back his hood, revealing

his ragged beard, bald head, and darkly glowing eyes.

"Marshall Webber." Frank glared at Batcho, who shrank back into his chair. "That explains a bunch."

The lawman Frank had killed glared down from the bench, his displeasure with the task at hand clear in his bottomless eyes.

"Thus, Frank Butcher, as much as it displeases me, I must pronounce you free and clear to leave here and spend eternity in a place where your pain and guilt will be wiped away. You will be happy, for the first time since you killed your father. Your suffering has reached its end."

Frank thought a moment, his heart sinking even further. He'd passed the judges' tests, but failed his own. Part of him wanted to leave here, to forget and be at peace, as they said. Another part knew that would be injustice of the worst kind. He'd killed his father and his only son. No judgment from these three would ever make that right. Nothing would erase the midnight cloud descended on his soul.

"Your honors, might I confer with my attorney?"

The three exchanged confused glances, the corners of Webber's mouth curling up. They nodded as one.

Frank leaned close to Batcho and whispered in his ear. "Do the rules of the underworld still apply here?"

"Yes, of course."

"So, if I die here right now, I'm stuck in this underworld?"

The Indian nodded, confused.

Frank straightened. His path stretched clear before him now, the doubt and confusion erased. He knew what he had to do, that there was only one way to right the wrongs of his past. "Your honors, no test can clear me of what I've done. I killed four innocent men, one of them my own son. I beat my wife, hurt many others along the way.

"You call my first kill, shooting my father, justified. That may be, but what's unjustified is that I didn't keep him dead. He lived in me all these years. I killed the man, but not his evil. In a way, I helped him kill my son. I don't deserve forgiveness or happiness, and I sure shouldn't ever forget. So, I have one question for the court, if you'll allow it."

"Ask," came their layered response.

"Did my father pass his tests?"

A pause. He'd caught the judges off balance. They conferred for a single, hissing moment, then turned their fiery glares back to Frank

"No," said Webber, his eyes hot as embers. "Your father spends eternity reliving in agony the harm he did to others. Including the harm he did to you and to your mother."

Webber waved to the bailiff, who tugged the black cover off the frame behind the bench. Frank gasped. His father's face stared back at him, skeletal and deathly gray. Sunken eyes darted left and right, lidless and eternally open, unable to look away from what he saw. His lower lip trembled and the cruelty in his eyes had been replaced with something Frank had never seen in his father: fear. Fear of himself, of the things he'd done, of seeing the black in his soul for all of time.

For the first time, Frank saw his father as weak and frightened, and knew he would remain that way forever.

Frank had his answer. He drew his six gun and pressed the barrel up under his chin. The handles had turned bone white again, but it didn't matter. He'd made up his mind.

"Then I deserve no better than he got."

As Batcho screamed, Frank pulled the trigger.

EPILOGUE

Frank woke on a jail cell floor made of glowing, red-hot coals. The acrid stench of his skin burning shook him from darkness, and the searing pain on his back and legs made him jump to his feet.

He threw himself on a nearby bunk, only to scream in agony as shards of glass embedded in the mattress stabbed and sliced his skin. He minimized the pain by perching on the edge of the cot, his feet off the floor, the shards only stabbing his backside. Around him, the bars of his cell burned, miniature columns of fire whose heat he felt without even touching them. Outside the cell he saw nothing. Only darkness.

"You get used the floor after a while," came a wheezing voice from the darkness. "The ssskin on your feet will toughen up, and you won't feel the burn anymore. The bunk'sss a different ssstory. You'll never get used to bleeding in your sssleep."

Frank peered deep into the darkness, searching for the source of the voice. He saw nothing. No one.

"Where am I?" he asked. Something in his gut told him his plan had gone awry. Something was wrong.

"Why, in Hell, of course. Where did you think you'd go?"

A pallid, fleshy hand gripped one of the fiery bars, seemingly untouched by its flames. Shadows shifted outside the cell, but Frank still could not see his captor.

"I was supposed to stay in the underworld," he answered. "To relive my sins over and over again. Forever."

The figure outside his cell laughed, a coughing sound, tight and wet, as if choked with blood.

"Thought you'd outsmart the sssystem, did you? Well, you were almost right. But by the time you pulled the trigger on yourself, you'd already been forgiven. Redeemed. By shooting yourself, you killed an innocent person."

Frank's stomach tied itself in a knot as he realized what he'd done.

"So, I'm stuck here instead?"

"The punishment for sssuicide is the sssame as killing an innocent," hissed the being outside the bars.

Frank punched the mattress, glass biting into his knuckles, shredding the skin, and drawing blood.

"Oh, don't worry too much," said the mysterious shadow. "You didn't dodge any sssuffering. They don't call it Hell for nothing."

"I was meant to relive my mistakes forever," Frank said. "It's the only way to find justice for what I did."

His captor moved, a heavy, sliding sound like flesh being dragged across stone.

"You don't understand. Justice was already done when the judgesss absolved you. But you messed that up. The judgesss aren't happy with you, and neither is the Bossss. If it's justice you're looking for, you'll find plenty here. Probably more than you wanted. This place will make the underworld look like a picnic."

A chitinous, clicking sound told Frank his captor was leaving, and Frank's sentence of suffering beginning. He opened himself to it, relishing the pain and welcoming the agony. He deserved all of it.

Smiling, he stepped off the bed and screamed.

HELL'S MARSHAL

Book One of the Hell's Butcher Series

Gunfighter Frank Butcher is in Hell, and that's where he wants to stay. Unable to forgive himself for killing his father and his only son when he was alive, Frank wants nothing more than to spend eternity suffering. When the soul of Jesse James escapes from Hell and picks up where he left off in the living world, the judges of the underworld send Frank to bring him back. But James has a darker purpose than just robbery and trouble-making, meaning Frank and his misfit posse must send the killer back to Hell before he plunges the United States into war.

Enjoy Chapter One here:

HELL'S MARSHAL

CHAPTER ONE

Turned out Hell looked a lot like a jail cell, only with bars of fire and a mattress stuffed with shards of glass. Frank Butcher hated the time he spent in his cell, even though the only alternative was the pit of fire they threw him in for punishment on a regular basis. At least he felt like he deserved those periods of horrific and agonizing pain, like they were just punishment for the things he'd done. For the people he'd killed.

One in particular. For Ron.

In the fires, only sheer agony and terror filled his mind, eclipsing all else and making it impossible to even think. Here, in the broiling cell, his mind had space to wander, to make trips back to the things he'd done that put him here. That was the Devil's way of torturing him, by dragging him back to the past and making him relive the most horrible of his deeds. A constant reminder he'd hurt people, robbed innocents of their lives, and killed the one person he, as a father, should never have harmed.

The fires cleansed him of those memories, wiped him clean for however long they lasted—Hell stole his sense of time—but returning to his cell always re-caked his soul with the filth of murder.

No, Frank would take the searing, purging agony of the fire pit over this any day.

He paced the confines of his six-by-ten rectangular prison, his boot heels clacking on the hard floor. After taking off his leather gloves, he ran his fingers through the burning bars just to remind himself that pain still existed. Pain worked differently here—his body had died, so pain should have too—but he didn't care. As long as he could suffer.

Frank trudged to his bed and flopped onto the mattress. Pain erupted in his back as sharp glass edges and points shredded his skin, ensuring every inch of his back was cut. The sticky warmth of his own blood oozed into the material, causing it to cling to him when he shifted. The discomfort filled a hole in his heart.

He stared at his forearm, at the fleshy latticework of scars there, a net of painful reminders. Frank discovered the act of slicing himself by accident. While stalking his cell, tortured by his memories and guilt, he'd brushed his arm against a nail in his bed frame, and for that frozen instant, his pain had been all physical, his mind momentarily free of its torture and suffering while it focused on the physical pain.

He'd started using the nail, intentionally rubbing his arm on it to draw blood and cause pain. Only surface wounds, but at first, they were enough. Soon, though, his internal anguish overpowered the minor pain, and Frank needed more, something deeper. So he'd taken a shard of glass from the mattress and sliced the back of his arm, pressing deep and wincing, almost crying out, while the sharp edge bit through skin and flesh.

Now he had scars everywhere, not just his arms. His chest, his thighs, his calves, hands, and feet. A mesh of thin scars—the wounds healed overnight here—connected pain from one part of his body to another, uniting him in a network of suffering, a web of sorrow.

Frank's mind wandered for a moment, allowing the image of a boy to fill his vision, a boy with dark skin and a hook nose, but eyes that could only be Frank's. The boy—just short of a man, really—gazed up at Frank while a puddle of blood grew under his head, soaking into the dirt. Frank's heart broke all over again as he watched his son die.

Something skittered in the pitch black outside his cell, an insect sound, saving him from the pit of despair he'd fallen into.

They were coming for him. Finally.

The sound neared his cell, a clacking of chitin on granite—or whatever the floors of Hell were made of. A moment later, a pair of black antennae poked in through the flaming bars.

Part cockroach and part human, Damon's hard outer shell ticked on the floor as he rose up on the rear of his six legs. He wiggled his antennae, searching for Frank. His human face was puffy and swollen, and he never opened his eyes anymore, preferring the senses of the bug with which Hell had fused him.

"Frank Butcher?" he asked, his feelers waving in Frank's face.

"You know it's me, Damon. You know everyone

here. Let's go. I need the pain."

Damon flinched back from the bars as if their flames had somehow hurt him.

"No fffire pit for you," he hissed.

Frank stepped back from the bars, apprehensive. This was supposed to be his fate for all eternity. There'd never been a deviation before. Why now?

"What are you talking about? Is this some kind of trick?"

He'd never known the bug-man to make a joke.

Damon rubbed his front legs together as his middle ones unlocked Frank's cell. "They want to sssee you."

Frank retreated to the predictable pain of his cot, resisting the urge to curl into a ball on the glass-filled mat.

"Who?" In his heart, he already knew and was hoping Damon would prove him wrong.

"The judgesss."

"What the Hell do they want?"

Damon shrugged with his two pairs of free legs.

Frank turned his back on the jailer. "Then tell them they already judged me. They don't get to do it twice."

"It's not your choiccce. Disssobey them at your own risssk."

Frank shot him a glare over his shoulder. "What more could they possibly do to me? Tell the judges I said to piss off."

Damon made a tsking sound, and Frank heard him open the door.

"Very well," said the jailer. "Hul will make you."

Frank whirled, but an instant too late, as iridescent tendrils whipped around his arms and legs, shooting bullets of fire through his extremities and into his chest. Before him stood Hul, a featureless creature, roughly the shape of a man, but with dozens of finger-like, glowing tentacles sprouting from each shoulder. As they attached themselves to Frank's body, each one sent a jolt of agony through his spine.

An instant later, Frank lost control of himself, his arms thrashing and jerking, his legs dancing an obscene jig. He fought for command over his body, but every time he did, tiny shocks pulsed into him.

"Ssstop resisssting," Damon ordered. "Hul will make it worse if you fight him."

Frank fought a moment longer, but fatigue rushed over him and he gave in. To his surprise, he didn't fall. Instead, he walked, in spasmodic jerks and movements. Frightened, he struggled again, only to be rewarded with a series of shocks that left his limbs feeling like jelly and his mind scattered.

He surrendered again, and stepped through the open door. Damon started off down the pitch black corridor, his feet clicking on the floor. Hul moved behind Frank, and compelled him to follow. Frank didn't resist, couldn't any longer. His will belonged to the being behind him, the combination of man and Man O' War who served as Hell's torturer. As if they needed one.

"Looks like I'll go see the judges," he muttered. "Tell them to piss off myself."

Somewhere ahead of him, Damon's chuckle hissed through the darkness.

HELL'S BUTCHER

Book Two of the Hell's Butcher Series

Hell's Marshal Frank Butcher and his ragtag posse are back, this time wreaking havoc on the civilized east coast. Sent to bring back John Wilkes Booth and his gang before they can kill the current US President, Frank wrestles with what appears to be his destiny: killing innocent people. Equipped with a new gun that seems to enjoy killing, Frank struggles to keep himself under control. Meanwhile, Booth and his gang traverse his old stomping grounds, plotting to kill the president and re-start the civil war. Frank and his friends--with help from an unlikely place--have to stop Booth's plot, and keep Frank from losing himself in death..

SMOTHERED

A Supernatural Romance
From B.T. Clearwater

Annie Brown's life could use some renovation. She's in trouble at work, her ex-boyfriend is stalking her, and she's just inherited her late mother's dilapidated Victorian home in Denver. The last thing she needs in her life is a man, but when handyman Mike Tolbert comes to fix her dishwasher, all that changes. Mike doesn't exactly need the distraction of a relationship himself. A combat veteran of the Iraq war, Mike suffers from post-traumatic stress disorder. His wife left him, and he struggles to make ends meet while still providing for his young daughter. Yet something about Annie snags his heart and he finds he cannot walk away from her. As Mike and Annie build a relationship, they discover Annie's mother hasn't exactly left the house, and that she's willing to cross the barrier between the worlds to control her daughter's life. With the ghost of her mother haunting them, Mike and Annie face his PTSD, her troubles at work, legal battles over the house, and a deadly plot to force Annie out of her childhood home as they fight to keep their love alive.

ABOUT THE AUTHOR

 Chris Barili grew up in the Adirondack Mountains of upstate New York, but his service in the U.S. Air Force took him all over the world. He wrote his first novel in High School, and acted as Co-Editor of his high school literary magazine. He moved to Colorado in 1998 and has lived here ever since. He holds a bachelor's degree in English, and an MFA in Creative Writing - Popular Genre Fiction.

Chris's short fiction has appeared in anthologies by Zombies Need Brains Press and Sky Warrior Books, as well as on Evil Girlfriend Media, Quantum Fairy Tales, Zetetic: A Record of Unusual Inquiry, and The Western Online. He is also author of the dark fantasy "Hell's Butcher" series, and has published his first novel, a paranormal romance called *Smothered*, through Winlock Press (as B.T. Clearwater). He currently lives in Colorado Springs.

Chris' Website: https://authorchrisbarili.com

Facebook:
https://www.facebook.com/authorcbarili/

Twitter: @AuthorCBarili